F
COO

Cooney, Caroline B.
  Don't blame the music.   Pacer Bks
[c1986]
172p

Susan, a high-school senior, and her
parents find their peaceful lives
threatened by the return of Susan's
older sister Ashley, a would-be rock
star, an embittered, angry failure who
blames her family for her misery

1 Family life--Fiction   2 Brothers and
sisters--Fiction   3 High schools--Fic-
tion   4 School stories   I T

ISBN 0-448-47778-5

Grades 7-9
85-21727

Don't Blame the Music

DON'T BLAME THE MUSIC

Caroline B. Cooney

PACER BOOKS
A member of The Putnam Publishing Group
New York

Published by Pacer Books
a member of The Putnam Publishing Group
200 Madison Avenue
New York, New York 10016
Copyright © 1986 by Caroline B. Cooney
All rights reserved. Published simultaneously in Canada.
This book, or parts thereof, may not be reproduced
in any form without permission in writing
from the publisher.

Designed by Alice Lee Groton
Printed in the United States of America
Library of Congress Cataloging in Publication Data
Cooney, Caroline B.   Don't blame the music.
Summary: Seventeen-year-old Susan looks forward
eagerly to her senior year in high school but finds her
comfortable assumptions and optimistic expectations
of life and people shattered by the return home of
her older sister, a failed rock singer with a
bitter grudge against the family.
[1. Family problems—Fiction.   2. Emotional
problems—Fiction.   3. Sisters—Fiction.
4. High schools—Fiction.   5. Schools—
Fiction]   I. Title.   PZ7.C7834Do
1986   [Fic]   85-21727
ISBN 0-448-47778-5
5   7   9   10   8   6   4

For Beverly Horowitz,
whose idea this was

Don't Blame the Music

ONE

Birthdays count.

They count even if you're unconscious, or crazy, or missing.

Sometimes a birthday counts more for the people who aren't having one than for the person who is.

It was the twelfth day of my senior year, but that mattered only to me. Somewhere on the globe, my sister Ashley Elizabeth Hall was a quarter of a century old.

We weren't talking about it.

One of the things we do best in my family is not talk about Ash. It isn't easy. If there is one thing Ash excelled at, it was doing things everybody had to talk about. The neighbors, the police, the town—and, for one shining moment, the whole nation.

I took a look at myself in the mirror. A shaft of sunlight caught my hair and added fiery autumn tints to its plain thick brown. I was wearing a lustrous new eye shadow my friend Cindy had loaned me and it made me feel mysterious, like a woman with a past. I smiled into the old warped mirror and it winked back. With two centuries of reflections for it to remember, mine would not be the loveliest. But I could pretend.

With a shriek of brakes and tires, Jeffrey's car arrived in front of our house. The first leaves of autumn rose up from the gutter in a rustle of protest. Jeffrey leaned on his horn and stayed there.

Ours is an old, old street, with gnarled trees and dark stone walls that watched the American Revolution. They also watched my sister Ashley. That war and Ashley were the two biggest rebellions ever to hit the coast of Connecticut. I did not think the street was impressed by Jeffrey, whose idea of rebellious behavior was to honk a horn too long.

Instead of kissing me goodbye, however, my mother started up a new conversation. "I'm dieting again," she told me. "Do you think I will lose more weight standing or sitting?"

"We'll have to debate that another time, Mom," I said, laughing. "Jeffrey has taken a permanent position on the horn."

My mother's fingers caught the loops of my jeans. "I should get you new jeans," she said.

I adore clothing. "That would be wonderful," I said. "Have to go, Mom."

She did not let go. Her fingers tightened, the knuckles going white. "Mom?" I said. "Something wrong?" I knew what was wrong, of course. Ashley. A person's own mother would at least like to know if her first-born is alive on her twenty-fifth birthday. But I was headed for the first meeting of the yearbook staff, this morning before classes began. I didn't want the topic of Ashley to ruin such a good day. My very own class—planning graduation. Incredible.

Mom's chin was trembling and her eyes shone with tears. Jeffrey continued to lie on the steering wheel. "You have plans for today?" I said sharply. She'd be all right if she kept busy.

She nodded. "Swish and spit."

My mother is the quintessential school volunteer—everything from math tutoring to lunchroom monitor. She comes home damp from swish and spit (third-graders taking fluoride treatments feel honor-bound to miss the basin) but she enjoys it. "Hey, have fun," I said, and I peeled her off me and sped out to Jeffrey's car.

There is nothing between Jeffrey and me but a stick shift. His only virtue is that his car is more comfortable and has fewer sophomores in it than the school bus. Jeffrey grunted hello and removed himself from the horn. The silence was blessed. Behind us, my mother stood in the doorway with her arms wrapped around herself, as if clasping an invisible child.

At the corner of Maple and Chestnut we picked up Swan. Ours is a rich Fairfield County town where people commute to New York City to earn money to support their Mercedes habits and where boys are named names like Halsey Dexter (which will look good on a letterhead one day) and end up being called Swan because they have long necks and bobbling Adam's apples.

My mother claims that one day Swan will be very distinguished looking. I don't want to wait for "one day." I want a distinguished male admirer right now. Therefore I do not daydream about Swan.

Swan bent his neck and lurched into the backseat of

Jeffrey's car. "Hello, Beethoven," he said to me.

One day in junior high I was in a talent show. Actually I'd quit piano lessons due to a total *lack* of talent, but I got conned into playing my one decent piece on stage. It happened to be the second movement of the *Sonata Pathetique* and I acquired the nickname Beethoven. Poor Ludwig. He deserved better than me for a namesake.

"Why, Swan!" I exclaimed, noticing. "You got your braces off. You look terrific."

Swan grinned shyly. Faintly I could see what my mother meant about his future looks. Too faint to bother with, though.

At the corner of Leeward Lane and Pepperidge, we picked up Emily. Emily is stodgy and stuffy. "You going to join the yearbook staff, Beethoven?" she asked.

"I'm thinking about it."

"Yearbooks," said Jeffrey in great scorn. "Stupid stuff. Who cares?"

I did. I loved the whole thought. That thick volume, its glossy pages, the white spaces for friends to fill with scribbled jokes, signatures, and memories.

"I," said Emily, "will be advertising editor."

"Nobody would buy a thing from you, Emily," said Jeffrey.

"Always ready to encourage, aren't you?" said Emily. "Everybody will buy from me. I'll just stand there and obstruct the flow of business until they submit."

We all laughed. Emily does have a rocklike personality.

"My father says . . ." Emily went on.

I stopped listening. Emily's father is very important. Most fathers are in this town. Emily told us how her father (the brilliant advertising account executive) was going to work with her. I was afraid with his assistance the yearbook would have eight hundred pages of full color ads and no photographs of the senior class.

"That sounds fascinating, Emily," said Swan seriously. "I think I'll work on your committee."

The only reason I didn't fall out of the car is that it's very solidly built. We reached the high school parking lot. "I don't see why the teachers get to park closer to the door than we do," complained Jeffrey.

"They're older," I said. "They stagger under the weight of their responsibilities." I thought of my mother, who had staggered and fallen.

Two years since my sister's last phone call.

Money.

Send me money.

How my parents agonized. If they sent it, perhaps they were supporting a cocaine habit. But if they didn't, their daughter might go hungry. But if they did, how would Ash have the motivation to become a self-supporting adult? But if they didn't, how would Ash know we still loved her, and ours was still her home?

My early memories of Ashley are good. She adored me. I was her darling baby sister, Susan. She comforted me when I fell from my bike and scraped my knee. She told me stories on Christmas Eve when I thought morning would never come. Snuggled in bed with me when I had nightmares and the moonlight tortured the shadows on our bedroom ceiling.

But when she came home several years ago she was calling herself Trash, and the name was frighteningly apt.

Jeffrey drove across the lot at one eighth of a mile per hour, searching for the slot closest to the entrances. He does this every morning and every morning there *are* no slots near the entrances, but in the two years Jeffrey has been driving to high school he has not caught on to the fact that when you're the last to arrive, you park at the back of the lot.

"Hey, Beethoven!" came a scream. Cindy flew across the parking lot toward us, a blur of scarlet and gold. My mother refers to Cindy as the Blender, because she's always whipping at top speed.

"Hi, Cin," I said, forgetting Ash, Jeffrey, Emily, and Swan. Together we walked to the yearbook meeting.

"I'm quitting trig," said Cindy.

"On the twelfth day of school? Give it a chance."

"It's had a chance. I want this to be a perfect year. I don't want it studded with academic problems."

"I myself want it studded with boys," I said.

Cindy nodded. "You realize, Beethoven, that it's only 241 days till the senior prom."

"Deadline fast approaching. We have to get our acts together."

From eighth grade through tenth, Cindy and I dated easily and constantly. But something went wrong junior year. We were stranded without boys all year long. Now, twelve days into senior year, we were dreading a repeat.

"You know, Beethoven," said Cindy, "your hair looks fabulous. It's got fire in it. Red and gold glints."

"If only a boy would say that kind of thing to me."

"If he did, you'd know he was a pansy to think of it," Cindy pointed out, and we laughed, and walked into the yearbook meeting.

Shepherd Grenville is editor. She is stunningly beautiful, depressingly smart, wonderfully athletic, and impressively popular. Shepherd is going to Harvard, as she told us back when we were in second grade and thinking only about going to the bathroom.

Harvard has not yet agreed, however. Shepherd's whole life is built around getting into Harvard. If she only goes to Yale she will never live down the shame of it all. The thing is, though—ordinary girls don't go to Harvard. Even a lot of extraordinary girls don't go to Harvard. Therefore it is important to do something to make yourself stand out from a crowd of overachievers. When they're stars, you make plans to be the whole galaxy.

Shep arouses mixed feelings in me. Ashley had that kind of determination, and terrible things happened to Ashley.

"Attention, please," said Shepherd sharply. She stood like a picture in a frame: elegance perfectly packaged.

Shepherd intends to have the finest yearbook in the nation to show Harvard. I do not exaggerate. She told us this last spring when she was chosen editor. Of course the problem looming before us right now was that even Shepherd had not quite figured out what we were going to do in order to make this the finest yearbook in the United States of America.

While she talked I watched Anthony. Definitely the finest our senior class has to offer, Anthony is beautiful, smart, sexy, and preppy. You'd think Anthony dated all the time, because he flirts like mad and is always hugging or kissing somebody in the hall. But the truth is Anthony hardly ever takes a girl out. Only we confirmed Anthony-watchers realize this. I was not the only one looking at Anthony. So was Shepherd. I sighed. I couldn't compete with her.

"I know what we could do," I whispered to Cindy. "Skip the yearbook entirely and do a calendar."

"A calendar?"

"You know. January: Anthony, nude on skis. February: Anthony, nude delivering Valentines. March—" I might have gone all the way to December (Anthony: Santa Claus, wearing only the beard) but I heard my name being called.

Or what passes for my name. I really must do something about this Beethoven, I thought. Susan instead.

"Beethoven?" said Shepherd imperiously.

"Yes?"

"You will be music editor."

I forgot to be courteous. "There's no such thing as a music editor on a yearbook, Sheppie," I said irritably.

She hates being called Sheppie. I don't blame her. I don't exactly love being called Beethoven. "What would there be to do except get photographs of the marching band and the concert choir and get names in the right order?" I said.

Even with fifty seniors looking at me my mind was drifting. I was thinking of Anthony, and of boys, and rock music. I am constantly composing rock lyrics in my head.

Give me a crush.
Let it smother me
Let it cover me

"Susan," said Shepherd, "I know you can bring excitement and originality to the role of music editor. You have a streak of creativity in you that has long intrigued me."

Nobody looked at Shepherd as if she'd lost her mind. They just looked at me as if I were the last person in town to think of as creative. I was furious at them all. Did they think Ashley was the only interesting person in my family? "Fine, Shepherd," I said curtly. "I'll get to work on it. I'll have a game plan for you in two weeks."

Shepherd nodded like a general and turned to Emily to discuss advertising. "Did I actually say that out loud?" I muttered to Cindy. "About having a game plan?"

"Yes. Aren't you embarrassed?"

"Of course, but I'll probably be even more embarrassed in two weeks when I haven't thought of a game plan."

We giggled. "Want to spend the night Friday and talk about it?" she offered.

"No. I want to go on a date with Anthony Friday night. But if he isn't pleading for my body I'm willing to stay with you instead."

There had been no yearbook with Ashley's picture. At sixteen Ash quit high school and joined a rock band of men in their twenties wanting the life of free sex, drugs, and stardom she would never find in my mother's household. Ash got into things like setting fire to her clothing and living nude in a treehouse she built in the Congregational Church cemetery. Last time she was home—nearly three years ago—she had shaved her head. Very shapely if you like skulls. Instead of delicate gold earrings, she had mutilated her earlobes with large, vicious-looking screws.

How my mother had wept for Ashley. And because I have tear ducts of the same sort, we wept together. The Wet Duet, my father called us. He took out his grief with a wedge and sledgehammer, splitting cord after cord of wood—enough wood to keep a nation of Eskimos warm for years.

Shepherd was passing out old yearbooks so we could

see what previous committees had done. I leafed through one eight years old. Under each senior picture in this volume were lists. Cheerleading, exchange club, basketball, student government, drama society. I loved all that stuff. I loved my life, my family, my friends, my school.

Ash threw it away without a single backward glance. She wanted fame.

Not namby-pamby, turn your ankles in, take a little curtsy schoolgirl fame, but the real thing.

Million-dollar, magazine-cover, household-word fame.

For a moment she had it. A single song. Not even an album. And then it was gone, like a comet that flames but once in a lifetime.

Where are you, Ashley Elizabeth? I thought. Still flaming? Or have you burned away to nothing?

TWO

As if a Noah's Flood of memory was not enough, I was
the only person in the entire trigonometry class who
didn't understand the assignment. Everybody wanted to
tutor poor stupid Beethoven. I like to be the smart one
who does the tutoring, not the dummy who has to be
tutored.

Somebody was passing a note around the room. It
looked like Whit's handwriting to me.

I am afraid of Whit Moroso. He is the lead singer in a
successful school rock group called Crude Oil. I don't
know about the oil, but they are definitely crude. Whit
slouches in doorways, feet blocking the entrances, his
cigarette smoke claiming the very air. Probably makes a
market in stolen televisions and hits people with heavy
objects if they annoy him.

Cindy likes him. I can't think why.

Everybody but me read the note without laughing out

loud. I of course read it and couldn't contain my laughter and got caught.

"I am an alien from another planet," Miss Margolis read out loud from the note. "You can't see me, but I am having sex with your little finger. I know you're enjoying it because you're smiling."

The class collapsed laughing. "Susan," said Miss Margolis stiffly, "perhaps the reason you're doing so poorly in trig is because your mind is on such trifles."

"I don't think sex is a trifle," said one of the boys.

"And it's a relief to know where Beethoven's mind is," added another. "Up to now, we weren't sure she had one."

I almost enjoyed the teasing.

Miss Margolis said, "You remind me of your sister, Ashley. You don't want to follow in her footsteps, do you?"

The laughter drained out of me. I think I literally paled. If I stray one inch, one thread—let's be honest, one molecule—from the straight and narrow, I panic. What if I did turn into another Ashley? Perhaps it was in my genes too. After all, I love rock music just as much. Look at all the rock lyrics I write. "I'm sorry," I said quickly. "I'll study harder."

The class snorted. I saw both Whit and Anthony looking at me and I flushed. I know why I'm afraid of Whit, I thought. He reminds me of Ashley and her gutter friends. I wondered how Ashley was celebrating her twenty-fifth birthday. Had she thought of us? Had anyone baked her a cake? Or was she too stoned to recognize the date?

I don't even know if she's alive, I thought.

Once my father said the next time he saw Ash's name in print would probably be when we located her tombstone. I never knew how to react when he said something like that. My mother just cried.

After school I didn't go straight home. I knew Mother would only want to talk of Ashley and I had thought of my sister enough today. Sister. It had been a word of comfort and love. But now my sister was Trash.

I walked downtown for a Coke. The town has ordinances that forbid fast-food places. The local town powers (which include my mother, although I forgive her most days) say that McDonald's, Wendy's, Burger King, Taco Bell, and the rest don't fit into the New England atmosphere we all cherish. I personally do not cherish my New England atmosphere that much.

I went into Dom's.

Dom's does not have any New England atmosphere. It doesn't have any atmosphere at all that I can see. I sat at the counter between an elderly woman carrying a shopping bag and a cute construction worker with one arm in a sling. The three of us slouched over cold drinks.

"Hi, Beethoven," said a male voice.

It was Anthony.

"Just wanted to let you know I'll be ready to help if you run into any problems as music editor," said Anthony. "I'm going to be troubleshooting for Shepherd, you know."

Sheppie could shoot her own troubles, but I would come up with almost anything to have Anthony around. "Thank you," I said. There was no place next to me for Anthony to sit and I could think of nothing to say that would keep him standing in the aisle. The construction worker, bless his heart, grinned at me, dropped several quarters on the counter, and shifted to a booth. Some people are saints.

Anthony sat beside me. The nude calendar idea came back to mind. I squashed the thought. It was hard enough to breathe already.

Ordering a side of French fries, he said, "What do you think of Danenburg? She's supposed to be so terrific but so far Brit lit is the most boring class I've ever had."

Poor Danenburg didn't know what to say about literature, so she just read aloud from the assignments. She was pitiful. "She just likes the sound of her own voice," I said.

"Don't we all?" Anthony poured so much ketchup over his fries that they vanished.

"You eat your fries with a spoon?" I said.

He grinned. "Actually the fries are just a method of carrying ketchup to my mouth."

We flirted, sharing ketchup-coated French fries and sipping Coke diluted with too much ice. I felt a crush coming on, and let it. Who deserved it more?

"Want a ride home?" said Anthony casually.

Anthony would flirt with any girl. But he would not offer just anybody a ride home. Heart pounding, I said, "That would be lovely." I thought, this is Thursday. Perfect timing for Anthony to ask me out for Saturday.

He paid for my Coke and left a lavish tip. We walked out together, Anthony behind me, holding both my shoulders. He half massaged and half guided, keeping the physical connection he seemed to need with everybody. I winked at the cute construction worker and he lifted two fingers in a victory salute. The construction worker and I had plans, even if Anthony didn't.

Anthony took my hand and we walked to his car. It meant nothing to him. He was not capable of walking next to a girl without doing that. But it meant a lot to me.

We'd driven one block when he said, "But I don't know where you live."

"Off Iron Mine Road."

"I always wondered if there was a real iron mine."

"Oh, yes. My sister and I used to play there."

He stared at me. "Your sister? Ashley? I can't picture her playing anything but a guitar. She used to play outside, like in dirt and mud and stuff?"

"She was a real person once."

Anthony shook his head. "I'll never forget that concert she gave three years ago. I swear that was real dried blood all over her. I was terrified of her. But she was so good! What a musician! And her act. Like raw sex. Must have been weird for your parents."

"It was a little weird for me, too."

Anthony kept shaking his head. "You're so conservative," he said. "And your sister was so—so—"

"Unusual," I supplied.

"That's one way to put it."

"A safe way."

Anthony gave me a very gentle look, and for a moment I felt something beyond physical attraction between us: real understanding. I had been floating in a daydream I knew I was a daydream, but now it was pierced by hope. How often does a relative stranger understand a problem as intense as mine? Truly there could be something between Anthony and me—something that was . . .

But the moment ended too quickly to be sure and I did not know how to continue it. Anthony was totally occupied with locating Iron Mine Road. We don't have signs in our town. The feeling is that you should be born knowing where the roads are.

A rusted-out dark green car drifted toward the same turn. Its back left door was gone, and the hole was covered with black plastic that had torn and was flapping. The license plate was a piece of cardboard with numbers carelessly Magic Markered on. The exhaust pipe dragged on the asphalt, sending out sparks of fire and clouds of smoke.

"I hate cars like that," I said, shivering. "It's like evil, driving into your life."

Anthony grinned. "Well, you're safe in here with me, Susan."

Susan. Not Beethoven, that unsuitable nickname, but Susan. The real me. I felt very attached to Anthony, our real names holding us together.

We passed the repulsive car, which was having difficulty negotiating the curve. The driver was filthy and sickening. He was wearing several sweatshirts and the hoods were stacked up at the back of his neck, as though his heads were layered. His passenger was an emaciated-looking woman with stringy blonde hair, wearing a thin blue sweater and a necklace of pearls that appeared to have been torn apart on purpose, so they hung in silver shreds on her flat chest.

"Here's Iron Mine," I said.

Anthony turned.

Memory stabbed me like knives. I turned swiftly to glance behind us.

The emaciated woman in the awful car behind us was Ashley.

Anthony talked of twisting narrow Connecticut roads and deep dangerous Connecticut potholes. We hit one, and the car lurched like my soul.

I kept staring behind us.

"Don't worry about that car," said Anthony. "Driver's probably on something. He's going slow—we're ahead of him. Nothing's going to happen."

Nothing's going to happen.

The words of a person who did not know Ashley.

We approached our neighborhood. The road widened and a dozen houses sprinkled the rocky valley. Mrs. Bond was weeding her budding chrysanthemum bed, soon to be a shower of vermilion and gold. In his driveway Timmy Ames was trying out the training wheels on his new bike. Behind the house Timmy's sister was trying to sink a basket in the hoop attached to their barn. A kid I didn't recognize was mowing the McLeans' lawn.

All so normal.

Behind us the rusty green car wove a crazed pattern down the wrong side of the road.

I didn't know which would be worse—the homecoming of Trash or Anthony's witnessing her arrival.

Anthony's life was one of predictable wealth and position. His mother had been a Shepherd in her day. His father was a colleague of Emily's father, and equally successful. Anthony knew nothing of the underside of life. He probably thought having a sister like Ashley was romantic.

The real Ashley was another thing altogether.

I had approximately twenty seconds in which to get rid of Anthony.

Right now, I suddenly perceived, I was the woman of mystery I had pretended to be in front of the mirror. A girl whose older sister was a vanished rock star; a girl to whom Shepherd Grenville deferred, saying she was full of hidden creativity.

Dear God, let Anthony keep thinking of me that way, I prayed. "Wonderful of you thanks a million Anthony got to run look there's my mother in the door worried because I'm so late see you tomorrow." I flung myself out of the car, slammed the door hard against his last words and ran up the path beside the overhanging lilacs.

My mother, in the dark behind the screen door, looked confused. But not as confused as Anthony. Down the road the rusted-out car was gaining. Anthony stared at me and did not drive away.

I turned my back on him.

Wonderful. Wonderful ending to my fantasies.

Girl flees company of boy. Boy senses he is not wanted. Romance will not continue in this episode or the next.

Anthony drove away. I would have wept if I had not already been bracing myself for Ashley. I was going to warn my mother, I was going to hold her first, and say it carefully, but there was no time. The green car landed in front of the house. It did not actually stop, but just paused, as if my sister were just so much flotsam and jetsam to be dumped. At least the soiled person with the layered heads was not going to stay with us.

Ashley slid out of the car and stood in the gutter.

The green car wavered on, caught in its own nightmare.

My mother moved stiffly out onto the steps, her hands to her heart, her lips moving soundlessly.

Ashley, Ashley.

Her cry of joy broke the sense of nightmare. Laughing

ecstatically, holding out her arms, my mother ran to her older daughter. Joy filled me too. I guess no matter how bad the memories of past homecomings, a homecoming must always mean joy. I went to Ashley too, and we both embraced her, and we kept repeating the syllables of her name and crushing her to us, and feeling the boniness of her thin body in our arms.

Ashley did not hug back. She stood there, waiting for us to be done.

My father appeared and he too could not speak at first, and when he did it was a whisper. "Ashley, honey," he breathed, and when he reached his daughter, he picked her up, because he is a huge man and she was tiny and fragile. "Welcome home sweetheart," he said, his voice breaking, and he set her down.

"Hello," she said, rather irritably, brushing us away like mosquitoes. She walked on into the house.

It struck me that she had nothing with her.

Nothing.

No suitcase. No purse. Not even pockets.

Ashley had gone out to conquer the world. She had come home with literally nothing. We, with our eight rooms, our closets, attics, drawers, and boxes. Our three sheds, our garage, our two acres.

My very own sister did not even have a toothbrush.

Dad held the screen door for Mom and me. A queer thing happened. We three did not look at one another. It was as if we were afraid to see what the others were thinking. We were waiting. Waiting to see who, and what, this year's Ashley Elizabeth Hall might be.

THREE

I followed Ashley into the kitchen. You're not really home until you get to the kitchen. A front hall is just a corridor, but a kitchen is home. Even Ashley knew it. She walked slowly around the old pine table, its finish long gone from generations of scrubbing, and squeezed into the narrow place where the fourth chair was jammed.

We were a three-person family using a table that, naturally, had four sides, and therefore four chairs. But the fourth chair was just a place to set groceries on, or library books. Ashley went to that fourth chair like an animal seeking its lair, and when she sat down she sagged, as if all energy had left her forever. The chair was not merely an awkwardly placed shelf. *It was hers.*

This burned-out woman was not the buoyant happy girl who cuddled me when I was little. Nor the crazed violent girl with the shaved skull. This was a third person entirely.

The memory of her own chair was all she had for her twenty-fifth birthday.

"I'm glad you're back, Ashley," I said to her.

No reaction.

I sat down in my chair, next to hers, and leaned forward, putting my hand on her bony knee. "I've missed you."

Now she looked up. Her eyes were dark in an impossibly white face and the circles beneath them were not from makeup. "You didn't miss me," she said. Her voice was brittle and sharp. It went well with her body. "Any more than I missed you. Don't offer me charity. I won't take it. I'll just hate you for it."

I jerked back as if she had scalded me, which satisfied her. What a first sentence for her to utter! I put my hand awkwardly on my own knee and looked nervously at my parents, who were standing in the kitchen door. They exchanged sick looks.

But I too hated charity. I had not liked it one bit when the trig class offered to help dear stupid Susan. How strange, I thought. Ashley and I have that in common, then. Sisterhood is in there somewhere. We just have to locate it.

Because this was no rock star dropping in between engagements. This was no victorious career woman spending a night between New York and Boston.

This was defeat.

My parents sat down with us and I knew in a moment my mother was going to do poorly. Joy combined with nerves made her dithery. It was the kind of thing I could overlook, but Ashley never overlooked anything. "How nice you look!" piped my mother to the daughter who looked dreadful. "I've always liked pearls. I'm so glad to see you wearing pearls." She actually clapped her hands a little, to demonstrate how glad she was.

Ashley was utterly contemptuous. "The pearls are fake," she said in a voice that dripped sarcasm, just as the pearls themselves dripped in ugly tangles from her throat. "They explode when I touch them. Shower the fans with acid."

My mother gasped, too horrified to see the exaggeration.

"That's nothing," I said to Ashley. "I have rubies that throw knives."

My father grinned. My mother stared at me in confused anxiety. Ashley's face merely quivered. I did not know what that meant, but it was preferable to the sagging emptiness.

The timer on the stove rang gently. All the sounds in my mother's house are gentle, from the doorbell to the clothes dryer timer. I thought, *she*'s the one we have to worry about, with Ashley here. Not Ash, but Mom.

"Dinner," said my mother tensely, as though "dinner" were yet another appalling guest. She glanced around helplessly, unable to imagine what step to take next.

"I'll fix it," I said. "You talk to Ashley."

I got the pot roast out of the oven, spooned off some fat and began beating flour into it for gravy. My mother folded her hands like a little girl and put on a bright voice to match. You could almost see her dressing a little Ashley for dancing class. "Well, darling! How have you been?"

"How does it look?" said Ashley.

Mom withered.

"You look good to us, sweetheart," said my father. Dad is an electrician and a football coach. He has a tendency to talk as if he's in a perpetual halftime meeting. "You're alive and you're home," he said, as if priming her for a better quarter. "We've done a lot of worrying in the last few years, sweetheart."

If he thought that would thaw his daughter's heart, he was wrong. "I'm not your sweetheart," she said. "Or your team either. And don't try to lay some guilt trip on me just because you wasted your time worrying."

Mother cringed, but Daddy simply nodded. In his view you won some and you lost some and you never worried about a play that was over. "Were you in New York?" he asked.

How odd that would be—Ash barely forty miles away all this time! I had pictured her in California, which seemed suitably remote in distance and style.

"I've been everywhere," she said. "Don't hassle me. I didn't come home to be interrogated."

Why did you come home? I wondered. Are you desperate? Hiding?

"Warren, darling," said my mother nervously, "don't question her so much. She's been home only ten minutes." Mom patted Ashley frantically on the shoulder, the hair, the back. Ashley removed her hands as if they were dead fish.

"I think it's fairly reasonable for a father to wonder when it's been twenty-four months since the last communiqué," Dad pointed out.

"We don't share reasons," said my sister. "We never have. Don't shove me, Warren, and I won't shove you. I just need a little space. And tomorrow I'll need the car."

Her demand was so sudden nobody was prepared for it. I knew they wouldn't give her the car. I could still remember years ago a high-speed chase on the turnpike that ended when Ashley totaled the car. Nobody got hurt. I don't remember what punishment Ashley got, if any, from the legal system.

"Don't call me Warren," said my father, rather pleasantly, and rather firmly. "And you may not have the car. It's your mother's car. When you have a job, and you're earning money, you can buy your own car."

I finished setting the table and putting the serving dishes out. My mother found the harsh talk unbearable and compensated by getting even more bubbly. "Well, darling," she said to Ashley in a giddy voice. "What a good night you chose to come home! Pot roast, buttermilk gravy, biscuits, mashed potatoes, and green beans." She looked at the food happily, and I knew she rejoiced she had made a big dinner. What if Ash had walked in the night we had frozen fish sticks or ordered pizza? But pot roast with buttermilk gravy—that's homecoming food.

"I can see what you're having. Don't run through a menu for me."

At least she didn't call my mother "Janey." I changed the subject, making a real effort not to sound bubbly like Mom or football-coach stern like Dad. "You know what, Ashley?" I said. "It's my senior year in high school. I'm on the yearbook staff. I'm music editor. And I'm taking trigonometry, and British lit, and—"

"Music editor?" repeated Ashley. "How stupid. There's nothing to do except get the captions right under the concert choir photographs."

"That's exactly what I said, but the editor told me to come up with something innovative and unique."

"I've been doing things that are innovative and unique for years now," said Ashley, "and none of them would fit into a yearbook."

My mother definitely did not want to hear about any innovative and unique activities Ashley might have gotten into. "What a nice color sweater you have on, dear," she said. "I love it on you."

I almost gave her as disgusted a look as Ashley did. "It's the only thing the Salvation Army had," said my sister.

"Oh, honey, why didn't you call us?" cried my mother. "I would have sent you money! I would have sent you clothing."

"I didn't want to hear your voice."

Another chilling remark. Delivered simply, as one stating an obvious fact—say, that the Atlantic Ocean separates us from Europe. *I didn't want to hear your voice.*

Mom began serving pot roast. Her hands were shaking. My father was not looking at Ashley, but at Mom, and rather sadly. Suddenly I knew that my mother was desperate—frantic—for proof that she was not a failed mother. That daughter number one really was a neat little suburbanite underneath it all. But Dad knew better. And his grief was for his wife, not for Ashley.

I stared at them all, and I did not know where my grief lay.

But I understood something I had never thought about, or known existed. Our house was run gently and smoothly because my mother was fragile—not Ashley. Ashley, thin and tired and defeated as she might be, had the strength of ten. My mother did not.

"Where *have* you been, Ash?" I said, unable to resist the topic. "Detroit? Dallas?"

"Every city in America has a roach-ridden, urine-stinking motel where I have slept," she said. "I have peddled my act in every corner of this worthless nation."

I could see my father getting ready to defend America against the charge of worthlessness. We had enough troubles without bringing America into it. "You're in luck," I said lightly. "We feature hot showers and roach-free accommodations."

Ashley gave me a long assessing look. I did not know if I got a passing grade or not. But at least I was getting a chance, which was more than Mom and Dad got. She poked at her food. "I guess that's as good a reason as any," she said finally.

My heart ached.

Whenever my mother is upset, she eats. The more she heard Ashley's flat dead voice, the more she ate. She piled the mashed potatoes onto her plate and added enough gravy to float them out to sea.

"You got fat," Ashley accused her. "Fat people have no discipline. They're slovenly."

My mother sat very still.

My father sucked in a deep furious breath.

"It's only five or ten pounds, Ash," I said instantly. "I don't call that fat. I call it minor padding." I smiled at my sister, willing her not to make things worse.

"Oh, Christ," said my sister wearily. "You're one of these sugar-and-cream types, aren't you? Always finding the silver lining. Do me a favor, Susan?"

"Sure."

"Shut up."

There was a long long pause. Nobody ate. Four forks played games on four plates. I had rather hastily jumped to the conclusion that I, Susan Anne, would be the savior in a difficult situation. Ashley had rather hastily pointed out to me that no, I wouldn't.

My father said, "We're glad you're home, Ashley. We're glad you knew you could come home. But I am going to have to require you to be courteous to your mother and your sister if you're going to live here."

Ashley raised thin eyebrows over glittering sunken eyes. "Oh, you are, are you?"

My fingers tightened on the raised grapevine pattern of my water glass. My mother's chin trembled. My father's jaw bunched.

The telephone rang.

It sounded like a cry to battle. We leaped with jangled nerves. I had forgotten there was an outside world: other people, other places. Ashley had always been able to do this: envelop people so totally in her own personality that other thoughts shut down.

Dad leaned way back in his chair. Normally my mother would yell at him, for tilting an antique on two legs like that, but tonight she didn't notice. Grabbing the kitchen extension he said, "Yes? Yes? Who is this, please? Just a moment, please." He cupped his hand over the receiver. "A boy named Anthony for you, Susan."

Oh, no.

Oh, major league no.

I was stretched to the breaking point dealing with Ashley, ripped and torn with thoughts of my mother and my father and how the four of us were going to exist under one roof. How could I possibly talk with Anthony, of all people, right now? I doubted I could talk to Cindy, who

understood everything. But Anthony? Explain to him—
without sobbing and falling apart—why I had leaped out
of his car?

More than anything, I did not want Ashley to be part
of my relationship with Anthony. And I knew she was
girl enough, and sister enough, to grasp right off that
Anthony meant a lot to me. And somehow, in some cruel
way, Ashley would jeopardize that, on purpose.

And yet—suppose he wanted to ask me out?

Suppose he just wanted to talk? Boy-girl talk? Getting-
to-know-each-other talk?

You don't always have a second chance at things.

He might never call again.

After the way I'd abandoned him earlier, it was amaz-
ing he was trying now anyway.

"Tell him I'll talk to him tomorrow in school," I said to
my father.

Dad nodded and wrapped up the conversation.

I stared at the silent yellow phone. Somewhere next to
another silent phone, Anthony stood trying to figure out
what made Susan Hall tick. I doubted that he could come
up with the right answer.

Blurred with exhaustion, I was amazed to hear myself
say, "Where can I sleep?"

But it wasn't my voice. It was Ashley's, expressing my
thought.

"In our room," I said, thinking—*our room?* My wonderful bedroom under the eaves, with its four-generation
rug, and stenciling—that room belongs to *her* too? "The
bed is made up."

Her jaw fell. "You knew I was coming?"

I wanted to claim clairvoyance, but honesty won. "No.

I was thinking maybe Cindy would spend the night Friday and—"

"Cindy? The skinny stupid one with the lisp?"

"Ashley!" said my father. "I asked you to be courteous."

Already the scene had a certain familiarity, as if we had been over this territory many times, and would go over it again.

Ashley shrugged and left the room, slipping past each of us without touching or speaking. I thought of the parable of the prodigal son. We had made merry for the beloved child's return too—but what happens when the beloved child doesn't say she's sorry? The parable doesn't talk about that. Jesus figures of *course* you're sorry. Jesus, I thought, you blew it. Not everybody is sorry.

"Good night, honey," my mother called.

Ashley's footsteps made little padding sounds on the stairs.

When she reached the top the carpet absorbed the sounds and we could hear nothing.

"Oh, my God," said my father quietly.

"I was just thinking of Him," said my mother.

We smothered half-hysterical laughter and touched fingertips around the table, the way we do for special blessings at Thanksgiving or Christmas.

And that was my sister Ashley Elizabeth Hall's twenty-fifth birthday.

FOUR

When I finally went upstairs to bed, Ashley was asleep under a mound of blankets, her pitiful clothing a heap on the floor next to her bed. She must be sleeping nude.

Nothing of her was visible.

I undressed in the dark, as quietly as I could, but my nerves were too frazzled for sleep. After a bit I got up again and went into the bathroom and sat on the closed toilet lid and wrote in my journal.

Back when we were all going to counseling (my parents' unending attempt to survive what Ashley did to them with each return visit) one psychologist told us to keep journals and let our emotions pour out that way. My father never touched his, preferring his emotions unpoured. My mother hesitantly wrote about which birds visited the feeder and who voted yea and nay at the Board of Finance meeting.

But I really got into it. I've kept my journal for years and nobody knows.

My first was a beautiful blank book bound in flowered fabric. The thick expensive pages daunted me. I wasn't writing anything immortal, after all. Anyhow, the book was too attractive to other people. Cindy reached for it, wondering what was inside. My mother reached for it— even bare acquaintances at school noticed it.

So I switched to cheap black-and-white-splotched notebooks with wide lines, the kind little kids use to learn cursive writing. Nobody would think of finding anything there but spelling lists, so it is safe from peering eyes.

> *They say you're nothing but a quitter*
> *And it's left you painfully bitter.*
> *Left* you?
> *What about* us?
> *You think our life is marvelous*
> *Now that you've come home*
> *and made our lives a combat zone?*

I could hear it set to music: throbbing rock band chords and haunting repetitive melodies. I felt better. Rock always made me feel better.

It was my one secret from my mother. If she thought I was going the way of Ashley—heading into rock music for a career—she would lie down and die rather than endure it.

In the morning I awoke unrested, still ridden with anxiety.

But there was no need. Ashley remained an anonymous mound under the heaped thin summer blankets.

I pawed through the closet.

Some days I know immediately what to wear. I put it on, it's right, and I'm happy. Other days I change six times and everything is wrong and out of style and the colors are terrible.

Today, when I wanted to impress Anthony and wrap myself protectively so I didn't have to think about Ashley, I had nothing to wear. Nothing.

The crush came back to me, in shards and pointed pieces, as if it had broken on the rocks of last night's family upset. I held the emotions to me, trying to find the happiness I'd known sitting at Dom's counter with Anthony, while the construction worker winked at me and the ice melted in my Coke.

All I felt was more nervous.

And no matter what I dragged out of the closet, it didn't feel right.

I am dressing for this crush, I thought. I guess you have to have the right clothing to have a crush in.

Ashley moaned softly and turned under the covers. I held my breath but she didn't awaken. I scuffled my bare toes on the hooked rug and exchanged my green cords for a pair of soft pale gray cords.

The rug is four generations of hooking. My great-grandmother started it for this very room: sixteen by fourteen feet of cabbage roses hooked from slender cuttings of old woolen skirts and coats. When she ran out of energy, my grandmother took over, and when they were both dead, my mother even hooked quite a bit, although she detests needlework.

It was Ashley who finished it, seventy-five years after

its start. I can still remember her, the winter she was thirteen, lying on her stomach, hooking, while the radio blared and she sang along, entranced by the double rhythm of the music and her handiwork. I remember how all my mother's friends were impressed. Imagine a thirteen-year-old with all that determination, they would cry. I wish *my* daughter would tackle something with that energy and dedication.

Little did we know what Ashley would tackle *next* with all that energy and dedication.

At the time I thought I would never forget which parts my sister and my mother had done, but they all blended in. There was no knowing, now, which generation had done which roses.

I think I loved the rug as much as I loved any possession except my journals.

After my shower, I tried a blouse with lacy collar and cuffs, and topped that with a fragile feminine vest, and added a very bright blue sash, so that it cut across all that femininity like electricity in satin. It looked right.

Now I was dressed for my crush.

The only problem was—what to *say* to Anthony? "Pardon me for being rude, but we were all having nervous breakdowns of different types and sizes."

I ran downstairs for breakfast. Mom was making biscuits for Daddy. He loves them drowned in butter and maple syrup. I had toast and spread plum jam on it. The morning was no different from hundreds of others. Rock lyrics quivered in my brain.

I could hardly wait to write in my journal. I would polish the lyrics during Brit lit. One nice thing about being a B student is that teachers never suspect you of anything. They suspect the dummies and they suspect the brilliants, but we in the upper middle get away with anything.

Especially in Danenburg's class.

My mother took the biscuits out of the oven with a practiced grace and slid the spatula under two of them and flipped them onto Dad's plate. She looked solid and strong and capable. The kind of woman who was elected to the Board of Finance and was chairman of the School Volunteers Association. How could I possibly have thought her fragile?

Anyway, we'd all had a rest. Ashley would be better, Mom and Dad would be better, *I* was certainly better.

Jeffrey's horn sounded like a brass choir in the quiet street. I kissed my parents swiftly and ran for the door.

The terrible reality of the thirteenth day of school sank in almost as soon as I shut the door and Jeffrey headed for Emily's corner.

This was not going to be a day to think about crushes and Anthony and yearbooks.

This was going to be a day for questions about Ashley.

"Your mom called up my mom last night," said Jeffrey, his voice vivid with greed. Greed for gossip, I thought, chilled. "She said old Starshine is home. So how is the famous rock star anyway?"

I had forgotten that Ash's first rock name was Star-shine.

It threw me. I remembered now how idealistic she had been, how she truly did shine with joy and hope, believing that fame and stardom were hers.

"She's fine," I said.

"Really? That doesn't sound like the Ashley we all knew and loved."

As for Emily, she was questioning me before she even got to the car. Her whole neighborhood heard her first question. "I can't *wait* to hear all about it, Beethoven. Nancy and Karen called me up this morning before breakfast because they heard Trash was home and they were *dying* for details. I'll *never* forget that concert Trash gave here a few years ago. Afterward my parents said if they had had *any* idea that Warren and Janey Hall's little girl would act like that, they would never *never* have let me go to—"

"Shut up, Emily," I said.

They stared at me. I am never rude. I am never even mildly discourteous. And this is just carpool, I thought. What is it going to be like in school?

School.

I had never quite believed that our school had two thousand kids in it. Two thousand questions and jeers later, I believed.

Ashley would have loved it.

She had, after all, achieved fame. Everybody remembered her, or had been told about her. But not her music. Nobody could recall her one hit, and I'm not sure anybody even knew there had been a hit. Nobody remembered her painful, hypnotic guitar chords.

They remembered her insane behavior. The treehouse in the Congregational Church cemetery. Her clothes—or lack of them. Her bald shining skull and her horrible vicious language.

She was my sister.

I kept my chin up and I defended her.

"The final three questions on the quiz," said Miss Margolis, "are a gift. An absolute *gift*."

"Whenever a trig teacher tells you the questions are a gift," said Anthony from the back of the room, "you know you'll need three advisors, a computer program, and four weeks to do them."

Everybody laughed.

"Don't panic," said Emily. "There isn't time left in the period to reach the final three questions anyhow."

I took advantage of the chatter to scribble in my journal.

I meant to write my anger against the gossipy eager faces that had pressed into mine, but my anger came out against Ash.

> *Sister, sister.*
> *Oh, how I've missed her!*
> *I've been worrying . . .*
> *. . . currying . . .*
> *my memories.*
> *Trying to brush them into something sweet.*
> Oh, Ash.
> *Today's been a treat.*
> *It really has.*

Those aren't rock lyrics, I thought. Not a poem either. They're my soul.

"My mother took trig in this very room," said Anthony, "and in real adult life she has never needed a single fact you taught her, Miss Margolis."

"Thank you for that contribution, Anthony," said Miss Margolis, glaring. "It was truly inspiring."

"Any time," said Anthony generously, and everyone laughed again.

I looked over at him, but his eyes didn't fall on me. By

design? Was he trying to avoid seeing or thinking about me? Or had he forgotten me? My skin prickled, yearning for his attention. It was hard to focus my eyes in his direction for fear that he *would* look at me, and our eyes would lock and I would disintegrate and everybody would see it, and laugh.

How can I manage to be alone with him, I thought, despairing, when so many people are rushing up asking for hot details on Ashley?

Please God, don't let Anthony ask me questions. Let him be understanding. Let him see I can't bear talking about Ashley.

I stared at Anthony.

His handsomeness was rather like a shield. Like Ashley's loud music or cruel words. I could not see beyond it. It protected him from view, and behind all that handsomeness, Anthony could be whatever he chose, and nobody would know.

What an unsettling thought to have. I threw the thought out, like crumpled paper.

"Speaking of inspiration," said Emily, "why don't we read aloud from Beethoven's journal? I'll bet she's writing something immortal right this minute."

They knew about my journal? My private hoard? My interior thoughts? *They knew?*

Jeffrey lunged over two people, sprawling on Karen's desk, and snatched the journal from my fingers. I cried out as if he had cut me with a knife. He would read it aloud. He would jeer. I would be as exposed as if they really had removed my clothing, and left me, like my sister, naked in a treehouse.

Whit Moroso's hand, like doom, robbed Jeffrey of his prize.

Once Whit had it, it was gone. Even Jeffrey would not think of attempting to take anything from Whit. Emily made screeching noises and Karen giggled happily. Miss Margolis hesitated. She lets us get pretty rowdy, because this is an advanced class. But she was going to have to interfere and nobody liked tangling with Whit. Whit held the notebook in the air.

I was falling into the jaws of some terrible dark hell. The mouths of the class yawned open around me. There was nothing kind or decent in the world, and I was all alone.

Gently, Whit handed me back the journal, unopened. "It's white-collar crime you have to look out for, you know, Beethoven," he said softly. "High-class Jeffrey's the danger, not low-class Whit. Lesson for the day."

I stared at him.

"The crime," said Miss Margolis, "is that you have diminished your quiz time by five minutes and you never *will* get to the three questions at the end of the test."

Silence reigned.

We took the quiz.

Or rather, the class took the quiz. I had difficulty even taking hold of the pencil.

The rest of the morning was like one great final exam. There was but one question: Would I cry in public, or would I last till I got home?

It wasn't so much that kids were being mean. It was rather that *Ashley* had been mean, and my mother had fallen apart, and things were awful, and held every promise of getting *more* awful—and who wants a fascinated world to know *that*? I wanted to take my crush on Anthony and hug it to myself, and instead I was being pierced on every side by the general interest in Ashley.

Nobody else had an older sister who brought nightmares wherever she went. They wanted the details.

I didn't have details.

Just terrible raw emotions I didn't want either.

Their questions chewed at me, catching my skin. I began to look forward to lunch as the great escape. There would be more people there, with more time to ask questions, but I would sit with Cindy, and Cindy would be my buffer.

I headed for the cold-lunch line, which was shorter than hot lunch. Mrs. Finelli, who was once Ash's English teacher, said, "I hear your sister is home, Susan. I hope she's well. And things are going right for her."

I had my stock answers ready now. "She's fine," I said. "It's good to have the family complete."

"I'll bet," said Shepherd Grenville sarcastically, laughing to her friends, her fellow shining stars, who appeared behind me in the lunch line I had thought would be safe. "I'll *bet* it's really choice around your house right now, Beethoven. My older brother told me Ash was really insane. She wanted fame enough to stand on anyone. Kick anyone! Knife anyone!"

"Just like you, huh, Sheppie?" said Whit Moroso.

Shepherd does not like to be upstaged. Especially by a delinquent like Whit she would normally never even speak to. Shepherd fans glared at Whit. Whit stared back at them until they flinched and looked away. He really has a criminal aura. Not Shepherd's super-prep style at all.

"Thank you, Whit," I murmured. I chose a cheese sandwich and Lime Jell-O. We always have gourmet cuisine in our school.

"Any time." He walked past me without looking at

me, which I did not mind, because Whit frightens me. And yet he had stood up for me twice in a row.

It was too confusing to consider.

Shepherd said sharply, "Beethoven, how far have you gotten with your plans for the music division?"

I stared at her. Twenty-four hours had passed and I was supposed to be able to present the details already? "No place," I said irritably. I tried to think why she was attacking me like this, and then it occurred to me—Ashley. Shepherd was afraid some of that ugly crude cheap behavior would somehow rub off. After all, she had put me in a position of importance on her yearbook. Ashley and the Hall family might be infectious.

Yearning for comfort I sat down next to Cindy. My thoughts were fragmented and my body felt worse, as if I were coming down with flu. Cindy will make it all better, I thought, turning to her. She'll say—big deal, so they're interested in Ash. It'll be a one-day wonder. Tomorrow they'll have forgotten. And say, don't you think Anthony is spending a lot of time looking your way? Don't you think maybe Anthony has a crush on you?

Cindy bounced in her chair, patted mine noisily, as if she and the chair were clapping. She had a bite of my cheese sandwich before I did, to see if mine was fresher than hers, and she said, "Tell me all about it, Susan. I am like absolutely dying. You didn't even call me up. I don't know a single thing. Now tell us everything. Is she on drugs? Is she still with that last rock group? Is she all burned out? My parents always thought she'd burn out very very young."

I said, "I forgot to get milk."

I walked away from the table, but I didn't go to the lunch line. I left the caf and went down the hall. I walked faster and faster and then I stopped pretending to myself and just plain ran.

In the girls' room I rushed into a stall, slid the lock closed and stood there with the tears running down my face. The sobs came. Huge racking sobs as noisy as thunder.

No need to panic, I told myself. You can handle it. You're still Susan Anne Hall. Plain solid sturdy Susan Hall. You have to be loyal to your sister, and you're managing.

The sister who would consider it a favor if I would shut up.

The sister who didn't want my welcome, because it was charity, and she would hate me for it.

But also—also—the sister who years ago knelt beside me, kissing a skinned knee, murmuring, *don't cry, Susie, don't cry, Ash will make it all better.*

Footsteps in the bathroom.

I stopped breathing, as if I were doing something criminal and didn't want to get caught. Halting steps. And then a halting voice. "Susan? Are you here?"

Cindy.

I couldn't speak.

"I know you're there," she said. "I can see your feet. Those are Beethoven shoes. I know because I was with you when you bought them."

I waved my toe at her.

"Oh, Susan, I'm sorry," said Cindy, leaning invisibly on my stall door. "I didn't mean to be rotten. I was a toad and I know it. I was hurt because you didn't call me up last night to tell me. Everybody in school knew before I did and I'm supposed to be your best friend. I'm sorry, Susan."

"If you'd stop blocking the door I could come out," I said.

We stood giggling, sniffing back tears, and I came out and we hugged. "Oh, Cindy, it was so awful. You should have heard the things Ashley said to my mother."

Cindy patted my back, like burping a baby. "Do you remember how bitter my sister Elaine was when she didn't make cheerleading captain?"

Elaine had been a stupid jerk who didn't deserve to make peanut butter, let alone cheerleading captain.

"Elaine was so rotten to us my father wanted her to apply for early admission to college so she'd leave home a year ahead of time. And that was only a high school cheerleading squad! Whereas Ash told the entire state of Connecticut she was going to succeed. And she didn't. You have to expect her to be bitter, Susan. You have to be nice to her. Eventually she'll calm down. Elaine did. I even like Elaine, now and then, sometimes on her good days, for a few minutes."

We giggled.

"That was sweet of Whit to help you," said Cindy. "I've always liked Whit."

"Why?"

"I think he has potential."

"As what? A hit man?"

Cindy giggled. "First of all, he's unbelievably cute."

"*Whit?*"

"Forget that he scares you. Take a look at his profile and his bod."

"You've given this a lot of thought," I told her.

Cindy shrugged. "I give all persons of the male persuasion a lot of thought. Now don't worry about Ashley so much, okay? It'll work out."

She was thinking of Elaine. But Elaine just wanted to be cheerleading captain so the boys would go after her more. Ashley wanted twenty thousand screaming fans to watch her walk onto a stage. It's not the same league and the bitterness would not be the same level. "I guess you're right," I said, because Cindy was my friend.

"Of course I am. You'll see. After all, you two have the same genes. She can't be *that* bad."

FIVE

One more class to go and I'd be released from school.
Like the end of a prison sentence.

I slid into Brit lit.

Anthony slid into the seat next to me.

If the space shuttle had landed there, I could not have
been more surprised. We don't have assigned seats, but
everyone tends to sit in the same place each day. Some
people like back corners, some people like the middle
and nobody ever likes the front. I was in front because I
had come late from the girls' room. Anthony, who invari-
ably takes the back middle where he can survey everybody else, had no reason to sit by me. Nobody would
ever think of taking Anthony's favorite seat away from
him.

I forgot Ashley.

All I could think of was that I had not brushed my hair
or checked my eye makeup after weeping in the

bathroom. What if I had mascara tracks down my cheeks?

Mrs. Danenburg read aloud from Chaucer.

Anthony passed me a note.

It said, *Want to go to creamcakes after school?*

Creamcakes, with a small c, was a strange little restaurant. A boutique, really, filled with sachets, lace, and ribbons. It served a fragile little meal it referred to as "real English tea." I could not imagine Anthony or any other real boy going into *creamcakes*. It was so completely an elderly woman's kind of place.

And yet—it was awfully romantic, in a delicate frothy sort of way.

A first date, I thought. At *creamcakes!*

I was afraid to react. Mrs. Danenburg might notice. The world might notice. I had to think about it by myself. Because this meant that not only did I have a crush on Anthony, but Anthony had a crush on me.

In the great lottery of life, my sister Ashley had drawn one thousand percent of the family poise. She could do anything in public. I couldn't even turn my head, smile and murmur, "Love to."

After a long time I managed to face Anthony, nod, and put on a reasonable facsimile of a smile. It felt crimped and false. But Anthony grinned cheerfully and nodded back.

Whatever Chaucer and Mrs. Danenburg had said together, I missed. When class finally ended, I had done nothing except think up rock lyrics involving Anthony. Anthony is a very difficult word to rhyme.

Anthony walked me to my locker. He helped put my books in my bookbag. And then he actually carried my bookbag. I was already trying out my name with his.

Anthony Fielding. Susan Hall Fielding. Susan Fielding. I liked it.

Anthony had a Mercedes. Everyone in his family has a Mercedes. Anthony's is silver gray. That way he can distinguish it from his mother's, which is dark gray, his father's, which is black, and his sister's, which is cream. If I had a Mercedes, it would be scarlet and it would flash in the sun and everybody would recognize me.

I'll marry Anthony, I thought, and be rich and drive a Mercedes.

We passed Whit Moroso and one of his band mates, Carmine. Whit was his usual expressionless self, dark, and looking like someone with secrets to match. As for Carmine, he has truly awful acne, as if something exploded in his skin.

Carmine didn't look at us. Whit did. He raised his eyebrows at me, as if there was something quite amusing about seeing me with Anthony. It made me mad. Why did I have two debts to Whit Moroso, of all people?

Anthony guided me across the parking lot to his Mercedes. I had spotted it anyway. Even in a school this rich, very few seventeen-year-olds have their own Mercedes.

And I spotted, too late to hide my feelings, Shepherd Grenville in the front seat. "Hi, Beethoven!" she cried, waving out the open window. "I'm glad you could come along. We have *so* much to talk about."

"Hop in, Beethoven," said Anthony, smiling, opening the back door.

Well, that explained why we were going to *creamcakes*. It was Shepherd's kind of place. Elegant, expensive, sophisticated.

I wanted to die.

I had practically married myself off to Anthony and I

was nothing more than an arrangement he had made for Shepherd.

Shepherd turned in the front seat and rested a beautiful slender hand on the leather upholstery. Her fingernails were perfect. A single narrow bracelet shimmering with green stones—which might even have been emeralds, knowing Shepherd—hung from her wrist.

She smiled at me. She knew, and I knew that she knew, that I had thought Anthony was asking me out. She had planned the afternoon that way.

Shepherd Grenville, you scum, I thought. You ought to have a complexion like Carmine's, and he should have your peaches and cream.

Shepherd was getting her revenge for what Whit Moroso said to her. Sheppie wouldn't dare try for revenge on Whit himself. She was probably as afraid of Whit as I was. But who would have expected Sheppie to be the revenge type? You would think someone who had everything wouldn't need to bother.

Anthony caught Shepherd's smile but apparently not the meaning behind it and said to me, "So how's the game plan for music editor coming along?"

"Anthony, I only got appointed twenty-four hours ago."

"But I have so much planning ahead," put in Shepherd gently. Explaining the complexities to the slow of mind. "I really do need to know how many pages you're going to want, Beethoven."

Anthony found a parking space right in front of *creamcakes*. He led that kind of life. There were always free spaces waiting for Anthony, instead of Anthony waiting for free spaces.

If I let Shepherd take control, she would make a fool

out of me in front of Anthony. I could not bear it. "Let's put off serious talk until we've had a chance to order," I suggested, ushering the three of us into *creamcakes* and choosing the table myself. What if Shepherd chose not to follow me? I would be stranded. They would head for another table and I would have to stumble after them and mutter apologies and look stupid.

But they followed me.

The table was tiny, because the amount of food they planned to serve was so tiny. *Creamcakes* was not a place for your typical adolescent appetite. It was for people like my mother, on the twenty-fifth year of their diets. However, the arrangement meant I was very very close to Anthony.

He smiled at me happily. Did he have any idea what was passing between me and Shepherd? Sometimes I don't think boys can read anything but words. And maybe not even those.

"I hear your sister is home," said Anthony. No prying. His voice was its usual light friendly self.

"Yes. She arrived unexpectedly right after you dropped me at home." I wedged that in to see how Sheppie reacted. She reacted wonderfully, with an almost-glare at Anthony that she instantly disguised as a smile. "How sweet of you to give Beethoven a ride home," said Shepherd. And if he did anything as sweet as that again, she would put a knife between his ribs. I was beginning to enjoy myself. Me, Susan Hall, a threat to Shepherd Grenville. *Mirabile dictu.*

"I imagine life in this little burg will perk up now," observed Shepherd. "Ashley won't let us all lie around in a stupor."

"My goodness, Shepherd," I teased. "All this time

you've been lying around in a stupor? And here I thought you led an exciting life. Cheer up. Ashley gives lessons. Drop by sometime for a free demonstration."

Anthony laughed.

Shepherd pretended to laugh.

Instead of basking in reflected glory, I was getting in a few sharp digs of my own. It made the day I'd endured—and the evening I would face when I got home—a little less awful.

A waitress trundled up with a tiny silvery cart covered with a lace cloth and plates of tiny baked delicacies. We each took one. Shepherd nibbled hers. Anthony swallowed his whole. Shepherd said, "Soo, Beethoven. Any thoughts?" She steepled her fingers in front of her, knowing I had no thoughts at all, especially on innovative yearbook ideas.

"Because if you don't think you're going to be able to come up with something, we have a volunteer to take your place. It wouldn't be any problem, Beethoven. You mustn't worry about it."

I rarely feel anger. It's just not one of my emotions. Ashley got all that, along with the poise. I had not, after all, intended to be music editor. I certainly had enough to do senior year without that burden. But Shepherd was not talking yearbooks here, nor her entrance into Harvard. No. Dull little Beethoven, whom she had chosen, I now saw, just *because* I would not outshine her—dull little Beethoven apparently had enough luster to make Anthony notice.

So she wanted me out.

And she wanted me to go out the door with my shoulders hunched in shame, admitting I wasn't able to do the job. Admitting it in front of Anthony.

"That's very thoughtful of you, Shepherd," I said. "Senior year *is* going to be demanding. It's sweet of you to be concerned with whether I can manage it all."

Anthony did not detect any sarcasm whatsoever. Boys are quite thick. Even unbelievably cute ones like Anthony. He nodded with me, saying earnestly, "Absolutely. I mean, what's the point if it's no fun? If it's just a burden?"

"Oh, exactly. I totally agree, Anthony. But you know, I think I'm going to have a wonderful time." I tacked a happy smile on my face. "I'm already deep into stage one." I took a bite of pastry. No matter how dainty I tried to be, that miniature excuse for food could not be stretched more than four bites. Stage one, I thought desperately. What on earth can stage one be?

I remembered the raised eyebrows of Whit Moroso— the contemptuous amusement he felt at the sight of me with Anthony. My cheeks burned. Words came right out of my mouth, without my considering them at all. "I'm going to interview all the members of the various high school rock bands. Crude Oil, of course. The Slippery Six. The Broken Ankles."

"What a terrific idea," said Anthony, meaning it. "I forgot about all those groups. I mean, you always think of marching band, and concert choir, and that kind of thing, but of course, Beethoven! You're right! The really interesting music comes from the kids who organize themselves." He said seriously to Shepherd, leaning across the table so she would have to lean toward him too, "I think Crude Oil is a great group. Don't you?"

"They're a bunch of semimusical juvenile delinquents," said Shepherd.

"You're just jealous because Beethoven is the one who

gets to hang out with all those skanky dudes," said Anthony, "while you're stuck with my type."

Shepherd was not sure she liked this. Anthony had not said she was stuck with *him*—just that she was stuck with his type. She said stiffly, "It is a fairly interesting idea, Beethoven."

When you're hot, you're hot. Go with it. "You know," I said, "I'd prefer to be called Susan. After all, we don't want to go on hurting Ludwig's feelings year after year." I steepled my fingers and leaned to Shepherd. "So from now on, it's Susan, okay?"

I had never asked anyone to stop calling me Beethoven. Not even Cindy. But now it seemed imperative. As long as they could use a silly inappropriate nickname, I was a silly inappropriate person.

"Susan," repeated Anthony. "Got it. Won't make the mistake again." He waved at the waitress. In spite of the appalling price we all had a second pastry. I took my first quarter and nearly gagged. What had I done? I had committed myself to interview Crude Oil. Whit Moroso and his scummy friends and their cheap tough girls. Carmine with his gruesome complexion. Tommy, who used to have a Mohawk, but let it grow out a little, so now he looks like a man who cuts his hair with an ax. Probably butters his bread with an angle iron and doesn't write with a pencil—just sprays obscenities on water towers. And Luce, who drums as if his drums are victims and his sticks the instruments of torture.

I pushed the rest of my pastry toward Anthony. "Want this?" I said, and of course he did, and wolfed it down, and thanked me profusely. Shepherd frowned. I thought, I have to round up the Slippery Six? The Broken Ankles? Scary sick kids who straddle their guitars and amplifier wires as if they're going all the way with them?

Shepherd suddenly looked pleased with herself. It was not a good sign. She had something. "A yearbook, Susan," said Shepherd carefully, "is hardly a newspaper, you know. What are we supposed to do with interviews after you get them? We are not a booking agency for amateur rock groups. We are not doing journalism here either. You need to keep in mind that we are putting together a yearbook, Susan."

Good point. What would I do with my interviews? Even supposing the Slippery Six didn't laugh me out of the room—then what?

"I think," she said kindly, "that your sister's return has had an adverse effect on you."

"It hasn't been too positive so far," I agreed, and I too smiled. It wasn't easy. *Creamcakes*. I'd like to cream Shepherd all right. "But we agreed on ten days, Shepherd, and you're going to have to remember your commitment. I'll have the game plan for you at the next general meeting of the yearbook staff."

I smiled into her eyes. She had no retort. Crunched at her own game.

Anthony said how wonderfully it was all working out.

Anthony squeezed my hand to show me how much he liked it when things worked out.

I don't know which impressed me more—the depths of my crush—or the depths of Shepherd's jealousy.

SIX

When I finally arrived home, my mother was indeed at the kitchen table sipping her herbal tea, but my father, next to her, had opted for Jack Daniels. No sign of Ash. No indication that dinner preparation was underway. Perhaps we were going out to dinner to celebrate Ashley's return. Perhaps Ash had already vanished, as quickly as she had come.

"So how was your day?" I said.

My parents looked at me. Older daughter insane. Younger daughter thick as a brick. "That good, huh?" I said. "What happened?"

"What didn't happen," said my father. "Your mother had a doctor's appointment this morning, but Ashley wanted the car." His voice was very grim. "I refused to give Ash the keys, so she took a kitchen knife and went out and sliced through the fan belt."

I gaped at them. What kind of message was that? Get

out of my way, folks, or I'll cut you, too? I shivered. "Really and truly?" I said. "You're not making that up?"

"No, we're not."

My mother took another sip of tea. My father tilted his glass and glanced down into it.

"What did you do to Ashley?" I said.

"Nothing."

"Nothing?" I stared at them. They seemed so calm. "How can you just sit there?" I demanded. "Ashley couldn't get the car keys so she starts destroying the car? And you didn't do anything?"

"I drove your mother to the doctor's in my truck," said my father.

"You don't think it was serious? Her doing that?" I cried. It made my skin crawl. I imagined that fragile wrist, flicking sharply under the shadow of the hood, eyes glittering as she—

I shuddered violently. "You can't let her behave like that."

"What are we going to do?" said my father. "Spank her? Tell her she can't have dessert?"

I thought about it. Eventually I said, "Why were you going to the doctor, Mom? Are you all right?"

My mother brushed it off. "Just another infection," she said. She's always getting bladder infections and she won't talk about it, she hates them.

I said, "But Ashley—"

My mother interrupted me, setting the teacup down hard, and splashing the contents slightly on her hand. It must have cooled off. She didn't even notice. "Last time she was home we got tough on her," said my mother, remembering. "She left. For good. Without a word then or ever. *Do you know what I went through, Susan?"*

"Yes," I said. "I was there, remember?"

"You don't know!" she cried. "I'm her mother. And I never knew, one night, one minute, if she was dead or alive, or hurt or safe, or starving or overdosing!" My mother was shuddering almost convulsively. "I can't go through that again. I'd rather see the evil that Ash does than lie awake at night wondering if she's dead."

The evil that Ash does.

What a thing for a mother to say.

I wanted to call Cindy. Tell her everything, share like best friends. But I didn't. Evil? How could I talk about evil on the phone where we usually talked about clothes and boys and hair and boys?

"And when we came home from the doctor's," said my father, "Ashley had—how shall I put this—redecorated your bedroom."

My skin crawled. Had she used a knife there too? Had she sliced something in my room?

My lovely sunlit bedroom under the old sloping ceiling, with its tiny dormer windows and its pair of matching pencil poster beds? The portrait of my great-great-grandmother and the sampler that her daughter finished the month before she died of diphtheria? I didn't want to hear about it yet. Trying to breathe normally, I said, "I thought you were taking her clothes shopping."

"She didn't want to go. She said she'd wear your clothes instead."

I am a size ten. Thin as she was, I doubted Ash was more than a five. I could think of nothing I owned that would fit or appeal to her. I didn't like to think of my clothes on her. Immediately I was ashamed. This was my sister, and she had nothing but the clothes she stood in. Of course she could have anything she wanted.

"Brace yourself," said my mother, her bright cheery front gone.

Ash had been home twenty-four hours, and the bloom was off the flowers.

A rhyme, but I had no urge to set it down in my journal. "Where is she anyhow?" I said.

"It seems she has a boyfriend," said my mother. She used the word boyfriend as if it meant sewage. "He came for her in a van. Bob is his name. They said they'd be back later."

Could it be the greasy creature with the layered heads? But he had not driven a van. Nor acted like a friend of any kind. Someone else, then. Or some*thing* else.

"Go look at your room," said my father. "I'm sorry, Susan."

Whatever had happened to my room was bad enough they had not cleaned it up, then. Perhaps it was beyond cleaning. I went upstairs, with absolutely no idea what to expect. I felt like someone in a horror film, stupidly opening the door she knows leads to mutilation and death.

But it was nothing like that.

The portraits and embroidery were gone from the pale flowered walls. Tangled black spiderwebs hung like fouled Christmas tinsel from the hooks, molding, and window frames. The movement of the door made a tiny breeze and the huge black fronds shivered like dying grass. When I took a step into the room my feet crunched on splintered glass.

I forced myself to touch the hideous black tangle. It was cassette tape. Nothing but cassette tape. And the splinters on the floor were the clear plastic containers that had held my collection. She had smashed and ripped apart every single tape I owned. And I owned a lot.

My hands were cold.

And yet, it wasn't as terrible as I had thought. Cassettes were hardly immortal heirlooms. The portraits and embroidery were lying on my bed, undamaged. My clothing still hung in my closet, the old quilts still lay neatly in their sea captain's chest. She had simply made a statement to me, like the one involving the car. This room was hers too, and she was here to stay.

I drew a deep breath. Okay, I told myself, it's okay. It's nasty, but it isn't actually insane. It's a lot of hard-earned money strewn on those walls, but it isn't my life or anything.

I turned to go back downstairs. Thumbtacked to the inside of the door was the jacket of Ashley's one and only record. Her flash-in-the-pan hit. Ashley's face and neck, upside down, her features grotesquely altered, music pouring out of her slit throat like blood.

Had that ever been in style—that vicious evil kind of music? Or had Ash succeeded by momentary shock value?

Well, she had shocked us. I hoped it made her happy.

Today the fan belt and the cassettes.

Tomorrow . . .

From the street came the sound of an unmuffled motor. A van that could only belong to Ashley's boyfriend was pulling up. Holding the curtains at an angle so I couldn't be seen I peered out. The boyfriend was very very fat. I could not imagine Ashley, who had said such dreadful things about my poor mother's thick waist, being around such obesity. He was fat to the point of revulsion.

My skin crawled. I ran downstairs. I did not want to be alone when Ashley and this person walked in.

My mother was still clinging to her teacup. "But why did she come home?" she cried.

"A place to stand for a while," said my father. "To regroup. To get ready to try again, I suppose."

My mother set her cup down. She straightened herself up, and like a little girl repeating a pledge or a memorized prayer, she said, "I will always give my daughter a place to stand." It reminded me of a lot of prayers. A last-ditch attempt to postpone reality.

Very quietly my father said, "No, Janey. Not always. Sometime or other we will not give her another chance."

I hung on to the table. I actually felt as if I would faint.

My father, who has coached adolescents all his life, helping them through drugs and failed grades, humiliation on the field and parents getting divorces—my father writing off Ashley like that.

His daughter.

My sister.

He's wrong, I thought. She cannot be that bad. I said, "The bedroom isn't so bad. I can get used to tape on the walls, I guess. Maybe Ash and I can talk tonight and sort it all out. Don't make a big issue out of it, okay?"

Ashley walked into the kitchen with the obese man. All thought of tangled tape left my mind. Chins rippled under Bob's mouth and stomachs jiggled under his T shirt. She certainly liked her men in layers. If not extra heads, then extra chins.

I had no idea how old he was. I just knew if he sat on one of the kitchen chairs, the legs would snap.

"Hello, Ashley," said my father quietly. "Hello, Bob."

She smirked at us.

I gasped. "Ashley!" I cried out. *"What are you wearing? What is—is that—oh, Ashley, that's my sweater! That's my designer sweater!"*

Ashley laughed. She pirouetted before me, like a model on a runway. She had taken my best sweater, so expensive it took all my birthday money, and sliced off the sleeves. Violet and teal blue yarn dangled from the cut edges. She'd tugged the threads to roughen it. She was wearing my seashell earrings, but she had both pairs in one ear and none in the other. A thin length of leather was wrapped around her neck, rather like a noose.

Actually, she looked very striking, like a high-fashion model wearing things real people don't wear. Things that appear and exist exclusively for expensive glossy magazine pages.

My clothes, I thought. I found myself wanting the sweater more than I wanted Ashley. Was it wrong to care so deeply about a sweater?

It's just a sweater, I told myself. In the great parade of life, it's nothing at all. It doesn't matter.

It mattered.

Ashley smiled into my eyes and said, "I didn't like the sleeves that length."

"Two-year-olds behave better than you did," said my mother fiercely.

"Really?" Ash laughed. "I behave any way I want."

There was a triumphant glitter in her eyes. She had proven several things to us. She had the power to destroy and frighten. She might not control twenty thousand fans in a coliseum, but she controlled Warren and Janey and Susan Hall. I licked my lips. Ashley saw and was pleased.

"No, I think not," said my father. "I will have to ask

you to leave, Bob. We are going to have a family conference."

Bob made no move. His eyes glittered like Ashley's
and a dreadful little puckered smile appeared in the fat
jowly face. I was afraid.

My father stood up slowly. If Dad was slender or
short, getting to his feet would be meaningless. But Dad
is a big man in terrific shape. Bob decided to leave after
all. His flesh shivered and his clothing shifted. We
waited silently. When he walked out the floor trembled
beneath the thuds. At last the roar of the muffler told us
he was gone.

It was a nightmare. The grip was intolerable. "So what
are we having for supper?" I said brightly.

My parents looked at me in disgust. "We'll order pizza
or grinders or something," said my father. "But first
we're going to talk."

"You may talk," said Ashley. "I choose to remain silent."

"Then you choose not to live here. Ashley, we have
done all we can for you. Always. We have forgiven, we
have struggled, we have paid, we have . . ." My father's
voice trailed off.

"You have not!" She was on her feet, a tiny thing, like
an animal. She looked appallingly like the tortured girl
on her album cover. "You *never* helped me. You gave me
what *you* wanted. Piano lessons, because little girls ought
to play Mozart. Ballroom dancing, because little girls
ought to be graceful. I begged you and begged you for
the guitar, the clothes, the jazz lessons, but it had to be
your way or nothing!"

My mother shrank before Ashley's fury. Rage poured

out of my sister like something volcanic. Like lava, it burned my parents.

"No!" screamed Ashley. "You had this simpering little suburbanite in mind. You couldn't tolerate anything else. Help me? What a laugh. You never did anything but obstruct and blockade."

The room was filled with her hate. Hate I had never dreamed of. I loved my parents. I had not ever thought of them as anything but loving and generous. She's right, I thought. How can *she* be right? But she never got what she asked for. She got only what they asked for.

Were my parents cruel? Or had they just made choices that turned out to be wrong? Or were the choices right, and was it Ash who turned out wrong?

"I hate you," said Ashley. She had stopped screaming. She spoke softly, intensely, like a hissing snake, and the venom sank into my mother and father. "I will always hate you. I would have been a success if it wasn't for you."

My mother began to cry.

It meant hours of crying, because she cannot stop herself once she's started. I usually pick it up, like catching a yawn. But not this time. "Ash," I said very slowly. "There's one flaw in this."

She looked at me with loathing.

"You did have success," I said. "Remember? Your hit? You achieved it. Nobody helped you. Not Mom, not Dad, not expensive electric guitars, and not ballroom dancing lessons. You did it yourself."

"But it didn't last," said Ashley. The rage seeped out of her. She sagged in her chair.

"Why is that Mom and Dad's fault?" I said. "How can

you go on blaming them for what happened years after you left them?"

Ashley withered. Putting her head down on her arms, she melted like a snowman onto the pine table.

I didn't look at anybody. I felt if I met someone's eyes, I would have to be on that person's side. I didn't see how I could be on Ashley's side, and yet I wasn't sure I wanted to be on my parents' side. Maybe there are no sides, I thought. Maybe all three of them did everything wrong.

I was glad I'd been a little girl. I didn't have to shoulder any of the blame. Or did I?

Had I become Miss Sweet Suburbia so they would love me more? So I could fill the gap Ashley left, and take all the love that would have been hers as well?

My father, who has to do something physical when he's upset, began lighting a fire in the kitchen fireplace. It's the warmest friendliest place in my world.

Crumpling newspaper, Dad arranged kindling and added a trio of short split logs. He struck a match. The brief rasp of the match was the only sound in the room except my mother's weeping.

The fire caught and crackled. Flickering beauty filled the room. I felt safer. My mother's tears dried and she held her hands, and maybe her soul, to the fire.

"How about if I phone Village Pizza and get four grinders delivered?" I said. I have always felt that food solves the problems of the world. If I could order grinders for the starving children in Ethiopia I would. As it is, I could make a peace offering to my sister and my parents.

"I'll have meatball," said Ashley.

"Make mine sausage with extra peppers and onions," said my father.

I placed the order, spelled our last name twice, although Hall does not strike me as a particularly difficult name, and agreed that fifteen minutes would be wonderful. I set napkins around, with extras, because grinders are so messy, and Ashley actually got up, took the pitcher from the refrigerator, and poured iced tea for us all.

We worked quietly. After a bit my father picked up the evening paper and read the sports section. Normalcy had returned so easily and so completely that it didn't seem normal.

It's going to work out, I said to myself. We have to expect these little flareups. Ash just has to get all this anger out of her system.

Ashley added another log to the fire.

I glanced at the reassuring leaping flames, and the log seemed very oddly shaped, and very shiny, and I squinted, trying to identify it.

My mother and my father and I stared.

Ashley chuckled softly.

It was the plaque last year's victorious football team gave Dad in appreciation of all he'd done for them. The finish had caught instantly. It was burning like a torch within a fire.

"Doesn't it smell evil?" said Ash dreamily, her waiflike eyes fixed on the fire. "I remember it smelled like that when I burned all my records. Maybe that was the shrink-wrap."

And I had a terrible sense that Ashley had power of which we knew nothing. Power to remove our comfort and strip us of happiness.

Power to bring us into hell.

SEVEN

It was a fairly warm day, but I put on a jacket anyhow. The more clothing I had, the more protected I felt.

Crude Oil's members looked as if they just came off an oil derrick after six weeks of beer, no showers, and lousy weather. They were hardly going to notice how I looked. Nevertheless, I brushed my hair carefully, put on new lipstick and straightened the collar on my jacket. I looked rather sweet and innocent. Preppy. I had of course dressed for my crush on Anthony. Now I wished for faded jeans and an old sweatshirt. I'd be less visible. Safer.

Anthony hadn't said much to me today. Shepherd was standing a little too close for him to do anything but sneak a breath now and then.

My crush remained intact, smothering me without any encouragement from Anthony.

I headed for the music room, where Crude Oil practices most afternoons. The band director is very loose about letting kids hang around. Some years the music room attracts classical types and the room is full of cellos and rings with Beethoven and Bach. This is not that kind of year. The cellists are all afraid of Crude Oil and they practice at home.

The long halls were hung with artwork. Watercolors had obviously been assigned, and seascapes and flower bouquets were everywhere. Oh, to be art editor of the yearbook instead, and have the simple task of reproducing artwork.

Reproducing.

The thought tickled my mind.

Reproducing.

In the band room, Crude Oil was exchanging some very crude jokes. They did not break off when I entered. They just grinned, delivering the truly disgusting punch line just as I came up to them. If it was staged to make me uncomfortable, it worked real well.

Whit Moroso never speaks quickly. He stares without blinking. You can never tell if he sees into your soul . . . or has had too many drugs to focus his eyes. Sort of like Ashley.

"Hi, Beethoven," he said at last. "Slumming?"

Crude Oil laughed.

I blushed.

"She's auditioning for us," said Carmine.

"Lookit her notebook," said Tommy. "She's doing research." Tommy is a hulking blonde, very noisy, very pushy. I hardly know Tommy. I don't want to know Tommy either.

Whit continued staring at me.

He had a hardened look to him, as of someone who

works outdoors ten hours a day. His hands were calloused. He wore a logger's clothing: old wool shirts, their mismatched collars sticking up around his neck. Dark thick springy hair fell over all the collars. "So what do you want?" said Whit. Hard to remember he had twice in one week stood up for me.

I swallowed. "Well. See, Shepherd Grenville—"

I got no further. Utter disgust crossed Whit's face. He turned away and continued playing his guitar. It sounded as if it was hooked up to every amplifier in the state. It was nice, however, to find someone who didn't regard Shepherd Grenville with awe.

Over the din I shouted, "Actually, Susan Hall. Me."

Whit paused. Silence rocked the room instead. "Yeah?"

"I'll be doing a feature on the school rock groups for the yearbook and I wanted to talk to you about Crude Oil."

Luce, the fourth member of Crude Oil, laughed. "Yearbooks are for preppy types like you, Beethoven. Artsy-craftsy girls who write poetry. Boys who take the soccer team to victory."

"This yearbook will have sections on every kid who's involved in any kind of music at all," I said.

Whit found that hard to believe. *I* found that hard to believe.

"Like what, exactly?" he said.

I looked around for inspiration. The wall was covered with posters of Michael Jackson, Johann Sebastian Bach, and Dolly Parton. What a combination. "I don't know," I admitted. "Shepherd told me I had to be innovative and unusual. I haven't thought of anything yet, though."

Whit smiled at me quite nicely. "You will. And when

you do, be careful. Sheppie will try to take all the credit."

My mouth fell open. I'm not sure if it was the unexpected smile or his attitude toward Shepherd.

Luce and Carmine laughed. "Innocent little number, isn't she?" Luce drummed and Carmine strummed and Tommy began singing meaningless syllables and a meaningless melody.

"I never see you hanging around down here, Beethoven," said Whit, as if this were quite mysterious. I didn't quite tell him he was one quarter of the reason. "Here. I'll give you the grand tour," he offered. "Then you'll know what to include in your innovative and unusual feature." He took my arm and escorted me out of the band room. Luce and Tommy made remarks that were drowned out by their own racket, but I flushed anyhow.

We went into a small, ill-lit room, about as big as the average bathroom. The walls were wrapped in technology: dials, switches, synthesizers, dangling wires, speakers, and headphones.

"Electronic music lab," said Whit. "Ever been here?"

I shook my head. I detest noise. Electronic music is nothing but squealing and pounding.

"I'll play my best tape for you," he offered shyly. "I wrote it for Electronic Music II."

Oh, no. A course strictly on a par with cooking and business math. A free credit toward graduation. But Whit acting shy was more than I could pass up. "That would be nice," I lied.

He put on a reel-to-reel tape and dimmed the lights in the little room even more. So the lights, then, were for effect, so you could be swallowed by the music. Whit hunched forward, watching his tapes circle.

It would not do to show Whit boredom. That would be like showing fear to a Doberman pinscher. I had to pretend interest.

From the tape came vicious sounds. Not music, but sounds: unlike any I had heard before: and they had personality, and emotion. Sounds swooped and curled around the room. Words began: strangely warped words that changed pitch and volume. Slowly the words stretched into a poem and the music/sound slammed the words against what felt like stone walls. The stones were sounds, but I *felt* them, I *saw* them, they were so vivid.

Crush, said the tape voice. *Crush*.

It was about bones that break, spirits that collapse.

There was a sense of being chased. Caught. Dashed against something brutally solid.

Crushed, whispered the victorious enemy.

When the tape ended, I ached. I had to run my tongue over my lips, as if I had done something strenuous.

I too had written a poem about the word *crush*. How different my thoughts of the word were! My crush was joy and love and hope and boys.

Whit's crush was terrible. Physical. Final.

Ashley, Ashley, I thought. Were you crushed like that?

I saw her frail little body hurled around by all the people she had met, all the failures she had sustained. I saw her flung against the walls of every roach-ridden motel she had slummed in.

"You thought it was good, didn't you?" said Whit eagerly.

To his horror and mine, I began to cry.

The Whits of this world are comfortable with any kind of assault but tears. He literally went white. I fought back the tears. "I'm really sorry, Whit. It just brought back memories."

Whit was appalled. "You must have some terrible memories."

I could not share my sister with Whit, of all people. I reached for a Kleenex and found one and covered my eyes along with my nose.

"I don't have any memories in that tape," said Whit. "It was just an assignment. We had three choices. We could portray breaking icicles, or summertime, or being crushed. I chose crush."

I put the Kleenex in my jacket pocket. "I hope you got an A plus." And I hoped I would stay under control.

"Yes. I'm really good at this," he confided. "I love it. Both the technology and the music. It's kind of a game, really. You get to combine electronics and mechanics with character and music and rhythm and patterns and when you get the assignment, it's kind of exciting, because you don't know where to begin, you have to start from nothing, and—"

He turned his head sideways, like an embarrassed child. So much enthusiasm in his voice! More, I am sure, than he expected. Our eyes met. His shrank back behind his thick falling hair. He wants my good opinion, I realized. *He's* afraid of *me*. Afraid I'll slap him down where it counts.

I touched his knee with my fingertips, to offer something—reassurance, perhaps, that I was trustworthy in spite of being on the yearbook staff. "Show me how it works?" I asked him.

He smiled again. Nothing sardonic, nothing halfway. A wide, delighted smile. "I like to start with an idea," he said, leaning forward, putting his hand on my knee, so that we were doubly connected. "You got a line from a poem you like or something? You need a poem to get launched."

How weird to think of tough Whit Moroso searching for good lines from poems.

"Maybe something you wrote yourself," he suggested.

Never once had I shown anyone my journal.

I pulled out the notebook.

I handed it to Whit.

He opened the pages and read aloud, "They say you're nothing but a quitter."

Whit read it beautifully, his voice wrapping around the syllables. "Wow. That's powerful. But it'll be hard. I don't know what I can do with it. It needs melody, which I didn't have in the *crush* tape. We want something painful in here. But we want love in it, too, or else it wouldn't *be* painful. So it should be . . ." he drifted into thought, and began nodding and bobbing to himself, adjusting dials, moving plugs, creating noise that he molded into sounds, taping his voice, combining tapes, arching and stretching them. "Luce!" he bellowed suddenly.

I was so startled I nearly fell off my chair.

"Tommy! Carmine!"

Oh, no. Crammed into this tiny room with all four of them?

They came in a heartbeat, full of wisecracks. "She too much for you, Whit?" said Carmine.

"Shut up and listen," said Whit. He played what he had so far. "Isn't that great? What'll we do with it next?"

"Needs melody," said Carmine instantly. Carmine put both hands on my shoulders and shifted me like furniture to the only available corner and left me there. They proceeded to forget me. Nodding in the mesmerized way common to musicians, they began adding guitar, chords, finding notes, reaching for melodies. They especially liked the word *marvelous*, and they made it ricochet around inside the tape, like bullets in the combat zone of the final line. Tommy, who was to my mind the most frightening of them all, began working up a second verse. He might be failing English, but he knew how to write. *They say you've never known success*, he sang softly, *well, honey, then I'd like to suggest . . ."*

To think that such good creative musicians were trapped behind such scary faces.

I had to rethink all four of them.

And then rethink myself.

I don't know how long we were in the electronic music lab. Time vanished along with nervousness. We were caught in composition.

They threw out their first version. "Sounds like somebody slurping in a dentist's chair," Luce complained of Whit's background noise.

They threw out their second version. Whit thought it sounded like a leaky space vehicle.

The third time they had what they wanted. Throbbing emotional intensity that sucked up your thoughts, made you ache for the quitter, and for the family she had come home to hurt.

"All right!" exclaimed Whit, laughing with pride when we listened to the final version. "Fantastic." He grinned at me, and without warning gave me a one-armed hug. His face was very near mine and I thought— he's handsome. I never knew that. I thought he was scary and ominous. But the smile was as warm and good as Cindy's and his teeth had been through as many years of braces as Swan's. "Listen, Beethoven," he said eagerly, "we got to do this again. You busy tomorrow? Let's do another poem. I like your stuff."

I felt an incredible surge of pleasure. Four boys looking at me with respect and interest. Thinking, this girl knows what she's doing. Whit, asking me to join them. It made me giddy. What would Cindy think—square dull Beethoven running around with Crude Oil. Although with a haircut and different clothes, Whit wasn't Crude Oil: He could be competition for Anthony if he felt like it. I tried to imagine Whit in a suit.

"This is going to be a hit, Beethoven," said Tommy. "We'll sell a million. We'll be stars. They'll put our names in lights."

Tommy could not know there was no more terrible thing he could have said to me. For those lights—for those million records—my sister had destroyed herself. The boys hadn't understood my poem. But then, how could they? How could anybody outside the family?

I was going to cry. Bad enough I had wept in front of Whit. He might even have forgotten already. But I could not cry with all of them staring. I got up blindly, stumbling over Tommy's huge feet. "I guess not." I reached for the door knob. "Thanks, Whit, that was fun." I ran out of the room. Grabbing my books, I left the practice room by the back exit, rushing down the halls, out of the dim school, into the darkness that had fallen since we began recording. Down the sidewalk. And when the sidewalk petered out, down the strip of poorly mowed grass that was neither lawn nor road. My shoes were too loose for running and my feet began to blister. My side ached.

I could not believe I had done that.

Run away twice in a week.

Ducking behind hemlocks when car headlights appeared for fear it might be one of the band, and they'd see me, and laugh at me.

What am I, anyway? I thought.

And who is Ashley, that she can invade me like this?

I stopped running because I could not breathe anymore. I walked the rest of the way home. Two more miles. Much much longer than I cared to walk. Ashley is my sister, I thought, and I love her. She will always invade me. Because I will always wish her life had been different.

I crossed an intersection.

I stepped up a curb.

And I had the idea I needed. We *would* have the finest yearbook in the nation. Thanks to me, Susan Anne Hall. I *would* have a game plan to present at the next general meeting of the staff, and everyone would be impressed— Cindy, Anthony, Jeffrey, Emily, Swan—and Shepherd Grenville. Maybe even Harvard would be impressed.

We would reproduce music.

We would cut a record, and bind the slip jacket into the yearbook.

EIGHT

The next day I awoke with my crush on Anthony. I dressed for it, and carried it around with me like a journal of its own. But Anthony kept his distance. Or had it kept for him by Shepherd. It was a good name for her. She had the crook of her staff around Anthony's neck, and like a sheep he obeyed.

Anthony Fielding was beautiful. True centerfold material. I understood him well. A rich preppy: articulate, handsome, athletic, and amusing. He disliked difficulties, having met so few. Shepherd made it difficult for him to be with me, so instead of working his way around this problem, he simply dropped the whole thing.

It hurt.

But what really hurt was that Whit Moroso treated me with the same expressionless silence as before. After that intensely emotional sharing in the lab, there was nothing at all. And I had no one to blame but myself.

He had extended an invitation. I had refused as ungraciously as I had ever done anything.

What had the four said to each other after I fled? Had they laughed? Had they been upset? Had they teased Whit, and had he sneered back? Had they tried to analyze my behavior, or had they lost interest the moment the door slammed?

I wanted to hear that tape again.

I wanted to hear my poem as produced by Whit and Carmine, with Tommy and Luce. I wanted to try out some of the other poems. And watch Whit again, and see his eagerness under all that insolent casual facade.

I wanted Whit Moroso to like me.

For the first time in my seventeen years I found myself in the grip of two crushes.

The first, on Anthony, was traditional. Every girl had a crush on him at one time or another. He flirted readily and touched easily, and there was always the slight sense that he was encouraging you because he really did intend to ask you out.

But few had crushes on Whit. Or at least, few admitted it.

Of course Cindy did but I was not even sure what I felt was a crush. I only knew that I thought about him enough to qualify. Between thinking of both boys, it was a miracle I even remembered to attend class, let alone concentrate on the work at hand.

Only a week ago, I had worn borrowed eye shadow that made me feel mysterious. What a laugh. I was the least mysterious girl in high school. But to me Whit was mysterious. Or so different from my usual friends that he qualified.

Cindy, carefully staying away from the dangerous

topic of Ashley, did not know about the topics of Anthony or Whit. Since those three consumed my entire consciousness, it was hard talking to Cindy at all. My best friend! And all my turmoil was hidden from her.

My kingdom's the kingdom of lonesome,
If you're looking for heartache,
My friend, I have known some.

I was not sure if I had made that up or not. It had a sort of country and western feel, as if I had heard it once when I accidentally got off my usual rock station for a minute. I entered it in my journal anyhow.

When I saw Whit in the cafeteria, waiting for Luce and Tommy to get their hot dogs doused with chili and onion, he looked at me without expression. I had to talk to him. I needed his help and encouragement with the record idea. But he was unapproachable. I had gone back to being afraid of him. Game Plan Day was approaching, all too rapidly, and I could not make myself cross the cafeteria, or turn in my desk, to talk to Whit Moroso.

He isn't frightening, I told myself. You know him now. He doesn't bite. Just go over there. He'll be glad. He's confused too.

But I didn't.

I couldn't.

I wrote about Anthony. I wrote about Whit. But I never put their names down. In junior high Cindy and I used to do name games. Sitting in her bedroom we'd write pretend wedding invitations, or do spelling games with the letters of some boy's name—like plucking a daisy to see if he loved us. Number games to see how many children we'd have, or where we'd live, or whether we'd be rich or poor.

I could not write the names of Anthony or Whit. I had run into something too private even for my journal. Something beyond games. After a while I stopped writing in the journal altogether. Life was too confusing for words.

Furthermore, I was fighting a war on two fronts.

At home was Ashley, and Ash had brought out the heavy artillery.

She demanded money. Dad repeated that he would feed, shelter, and clothe her, but beyond that she was on her own, as a woman of twenty-five should be. Over and over Ashley screamed her favorite refrain. *You never did anything for me. I deserve more! You are scum!*

I didn't listen. By now I knew Ashley would blame anything for her failures. Presidents, acid rain, preservatives in white bread.

But my mother clung to her teacup as if it were welded to her fingers.

Ash demanded the car now that it was in working order. Iron Mine Road is really quite remote. It's a long drive to anything. My mother needs the car for every errand, meeting, and volunteer hour. When they denied Ash the car, she began a daily assault upon the car itself. She drained the gas tank. She left the lights on all night to wear out the battery.

And the dog was afraid of her.

We didn't know why.

Copper isn't much of a dog. He never was. Summer people who rented behind us abandoned a litter of puppies and this one had wandered to us for his food and water. Copper adores my mother with a slobbery affection that would drive me crazy, but I'm not the recipient. Only Mom. Copper flings himself upon her joyously a hundred times a day.

He was skulking around the house, hiding under furniture too small for him to fit beneath, so that his tail stuck out and his bent haunches spread obscenely into the room.

Bob kept appearing.

He never knocked. If you didn't hear the van, you weren't ready for him. Suddenly sweaty rolls of fat would fill all your breathing space. He didn't speak often. You never had any inkling of his personality, which made him all the more terrifying.

My mother took to locking up constantly—hooking screens, closing windows, latching shutters. Ashley, of course, followed her around, unlocking, unclosing, and unhinging.

In one week, my mother's mind was unhinged, too.

Ashley took my favorite sweatshirt. It was bright pink, with no hood, no pockets and no zipper: just a plain cotton sweatshirt. She slit it up and down all over, so that it looked like the construction paper lanterns that we made in kindergarten. She wore this over a bright green blouse of mine. The colors were very preppy. The result was like a sliced loaf of pink and green prep.

I stormed around the house, screaming, "It's *my* sweatshirt! It's my bedroom! Daddy, you have to stop her! Mom, you can't just sit there and drink more tea. How long am I supposed to keep quiet? Don't my feelings count too? How much can I take? You have to *do* something."

"All right," said my father. "Just tell me what to do, Susan."

"I don't know!" I screamed, hating him for his helplessness. Big tough football-coach–type men weren't supposed to be defeated by scrawny little girls with a pair of scissors. "Chain her up in the cellar while we're gone or something."

He nodded. "That would work. Unfortunately society frowns on people who chain their daughters up in the cellar. Very hard to explain to the judge."

"Then—then—" I gasped for breath, trying to find words for my rage, and ways to make Ashley leave my clothes alone.

"I can't cut her allowance," my father said. "I can't send her to bed early. And we're not going to call the police. For one thing, I don't know what charge we would bring. For another, your mother cannot bear the publicity. Ashley knows that. Ashley would make a scene so great she'd not only be in the papers, she'd also get the network television in. We couldn't take it, Susan."

"So we take this instead?" I shook my ruined clothing in his face.

He held me by my shoulders. "It's nothing but cloth. We'll buy you more. You're being very strong and I'm very proud of you. Your mother and I have made the decision to keep trying with Ashley. Maybe it's the wrong decision. Certainly any decision we've ever made with her has been the wrong one. But it's the one we've made, and you have to live with it as well."

Do I want to be that strong? I thought. Do I want to give her more chances? "What if we asked her to go?" I said.

"Yesterday," said my father, smiling sadly, "I told her I would throw her out. She said she'd just sleep in the gutter in front of the house. She would, you know. She'd love it. She'd get publicity for it, too. Every kid in high school would know that winter is coming and your poor sister is sleeping in the road without a blanket because of her cruel family."

I can hardly wait, I thought. Shepherd and Anthony asking me why we're being so mean to frail needy little Ash.

I wanted my best friend so much my heart screamed her name. *Cindy! Cindy!* But I didn't phone and I didn't go over.

And how could I tell anybody, even my best friend Cindy, the terrible thoughts that chased in my mind about my own sister? How on the one hand I wanted to give Ashley everything and on the other hand I could kill her for ruining my designer sweater, my room, and my life?

"I just realized," I said to my father, "that most people are rational. Fair. Willing to compromise."

He agreed. "Nothing applies with Ash. That's why we're so helpless." His face sagged like an old man's. "We failed, Susan," he said harshly. "A parent's task is to bring up children to be good citizens. And we failed."

The weather turned cold abruptly, like a slap. Indian Summer would come, but the ferocity of early winter gave us pause. One afternoon while Ash and Bob worked on his van in the driveway I was doing my trig in the kitchen. I imagined the house during the day, when my parents and I were gone. Were Ash and Bob there alone? What did they do? Who did they have over? Did they touch our things?

Ash had the radio turned up much too loud, but nobody complained. They were all a little afraid to complain. Ashley and Bob looked truly depraved: the one a shadow of herself, the other an animal fat enough for hibernation, grunting and sweating over something in his van.

When Mom drove up Iron Mine Road, she slowed up way down the street. She didn't want to enter her own driveway. I think she would have gone right past, and postponed coming home altogether, but Ashley saw her, and waved, and Mom did not know what to do but stop.

I closed my trig book, set down my pencil, and went out to give her courage. I went down the walk, past the withered lilacs, instead of using the driveway. Too close to Bob.

Ashley and Bob both had scissors in their hands.

Scissors? I thought.

Ash was cutting something heavy and dark. Bob dropped his scissors and began slicing with an Exacto knife.

"Hi, Mom," said Ashley cheerfully. "This old van is too cold for winter. We're upholstering it."

"That's nice, dear," said my mother, in whom hope springs eternal.

Cautiously Mom and I skirted the van, taking a look at the new upholstery. It seemed such a civilized thing for Bob or Ashley to do.

My mother cried out, as if in pain.

My first thought was that Ashley had used the scissors on Mom. I was so sick with horror I could hardly think, but when I stepped forward to protect her, I saw what had made her cry out. Chopped into pieces that would conform to the inside of the van, glued and tacked into place, was our four-generation hooked rug.

Our rug.

In a van where Ash and Bob would smoke pot and have kinky sex.

In her sweet voice my sister said, "You have a problem, Mom?"

My mother was pale. There were tears in her eyes.

I led her into the house. When we were inside, I shut the door and locked it, and then I walked her into the kitchen and I locked that door too and I said, "Mom, call the police. Send her away. Have her committed. Do anything! She is horrible. Let's admit it. Let's cut our losses now before something truly dreadful happens. *Ashley is diseased.*"

My mother got to the phone, falling, like a vomiting invalid trying to reach the toilet in time. Seizing the receiver she dialed, but not the emergency number. My father's, at the gym.

Her lips could hardly form words.

When he answered, she whispered, "Warren. *Oh, God!* Warren!"

The family conference on that episode was more like a war, complete with grenades and fallout. It was impossible that our loving close family—that popped popcorn together, and cheered at football games together, and never had arguments over anything more meaningful than whether to order pepperoni or sausage on the pizza—could have become this screaming violent quartet. If we had changed galaxies, the contrast could not have been greater.

Or more heart-rending.

Nothing was solved.

If anything it was worse.

We stopped the fight only because we were too tired to go on with it. Perhaps it would always be like that. Perhaps the war would come on schedule and stop for dinner like stopping for halftime.

That night Ashley and I lay in bed, both of us awake. It was a weird kind of slumber party. One blonde girl in her bed, one brunette across the room, but I was not ready to giggle and gossip.

"Ash?" I fingered my sheets. My mother had sewn row after row of ivory lace onto plain sheets, so that when you turned them back there was ten inches of luxuriant femininity.

"What?"

You had to be direct with Ash. We had learned that quickly. Nobody on earth had less tolerance for small talk and subtlety.

"We aren't getting along very well," I said, with magnificent understatement. "But we're sisters. What do you think we should do to make it better?"

"You are assuming," said my sister, "that I want it to get better."

I had not thought of that. Could she relish these fights enough to start them for the fun of it? "Of course you do," I said. "You're my sister and anyway you're an adult." It was a pitiful argument.

"If I'm so adult, how come I can't use the car?"

"You have to earn your own money and buy your own car," I said.

"If you're always going to be on *their* side, I don't know how you think we could ever get along."

"It isn't their side so much as I agree with them. You have to prove you can be good first." I felt like a nursery school teacher with a toddler who throws cookies across the room.

"My definition of good is different," said Ashley.

"You can't have different definitions of good in the same house," I said. In the dark I could see the floor. I had never seen it. My entire life it had been covered with the hooked rug. I thought of Ashley and Bob in this room—my room—lifting the beds, moving the bureaus, rolling up the rug.

"Certainly you can. You behave your way, Susan. You're exactly what they want. Second time around God filled the order properly. And I'll behave my way."

I am exactly what my parents want, I thought.

I tried to see that as a crime, or at least something undesirable. Ashley's voice told me it was despicable.

And then her voice changed. It was a real voice, for the first time. No taunting sweetness; no screaming rage. It was my sister, my real sister. "Oh, Susan!" she cried. "I tried so hard. I worked at everything. I learned all of it, every single aspect of producing rock music. I was willing to do anything. I did all the scut work, I slept with anyone. It never mattered because I was going to succeed. *But I didn't.*"

Whit could not have created a sound that held more pain.

I wept into the pillow and it sogged up my tears like cereal sogging up the milk. Ashley went on and on, talking and talking. Not a single good memory. Not a single happy moment. At least, not that she told me. It seemed to me she had wanted success the way I imagined a heroin addict needs a fix.

A future filled with fame.

If she could not have it, she would fill it with rage.

I tried to tell her that I understood, but she did not want me to interrupt her. I wanted to share something in return, but I could not trust her, and besides, what was a little embarrassment over Whit Moroso compared to a life gone sour?

In the end I fell asleep when she was still talking, and what she thought when she realized that I did not know. In the morning, I woke first. My clock radio comes on at six thirty. That morning at six thirty, the radio came on playing what seemed to me the last chords of Ashley's hit.

I sat up in bed, chilled.

Ashley did not wake up.

Had I just heard her own hit? And she slept on, not hearing it.

How strange, really, that we had heard no music from Ashley since she got home. Had it all been drained out of her?

The song was excellent. It had deserved its popularity. The DJ said nothing about it. Perhaps he could remember nothing. That group had literally been a one-week wonder, and that week had passed from every memory but Ashley's.

I dressed in the half dark, and in the clear light of the bathroom I nearly went into shock. Ashley had been at work on my clothes. She had cut off the buttons and shredded cuffs. She had painted an obscenity on the back of the shirt.

I still could not believe it. That she trespassed upon me

like that! How much could we put up with? To have my clothing mutilated, day after day! It was impossible.

But impossible, too, to wake a sleeping Ashley and yell at her. Better just to wear something else and shrug.

The radio played a particularly unpleasant selection of rock singers. Not one of my favorites. All of a sudden I hated it. Hated rock, hated rock musicians, because *look what rock music had done to our lives!*

Choking on screams of my own rage, I ran downstairs. My mother was listening to the local radio station for the weather, and they, incredibly, were playing Ashley's hit single.

We stared at the radio as if it contained the answers to the mysteries of life. I held up my arms so my mother could see the shredded sleeves. We wept together. "I will never play rock again," I told her passionately. I turned the radio off so hard the knob broke in my hand. I stared at it. Never in my life had I purposely broken anything. "Look what rock has done to us!" I sobbed, biting the words like an animal ripping flesh from a bone. "Look how horrible it is. You get into rock and it ruins you."

My mother held me, wrapping me in her arms, rocking me, kissing me everywhere, her tears damp on my cheek and neck. "Oh, Susan. No, no, no. Susan, honey, it isn't rock's fault."

"Then whose fault is it?" I cried. "Of course it's rock."

"I grew up on rock music," she said. "I love it. I always have. The Beatles. Kiss. The Who, Diana Ross. Bruce Springsteen. Donna Summer. Susan, a hundred names are filling my mind and a thousand lyrics are racing through me. I could list forever." She ran her fingers through my hair, tugging my head back and kissing the stains on my face. "Rock music has brought me endless pleasure."

"But what about Ashley?"

"Ashley twisted it."

"No, Mother!" I cried, willing her to understand. "Rock music twisted Ashley!"

The pain in my mother's voice matched Ashley's of last night. "Susan, Ashley was never a musician. She had no real talent. What's more, she had no respect for the music itself. She just wanted fame, and rock was the technique she chose."

I stared at her.

"If anything," said my mother gently, "*she* was the one who damaged rock." She poured orange juice for me, and pushed two slices of cinnamon raisin bread into the toaster.

"We're going to ride this out," she said to me. "Have faith, honey. Something went terribly wrong with your sister, and maybe it was my fault, and maybe it wasn't, but at least let's not blame music."

Ashley appeared in the door.

We stared at her. Her hair unbrushed, her face unwashed, her nightgown—mine, actually—crumpled. her eyes blazing. Filled with the hatred she had told us about. "Then who do we blame?" she said in icy rage. "Who do we blame because Ashley Elizabeth Hall went terribly wrong?"

We shrank from her. "I would rather not lay blame," said my mother. "I would rather work things out."

Ashley amazed us by quoting the Bible. She had gone to Sunday school, but who would have thought anything stuck? "You think you can make the rough places plain, Mother, and the crooked straight? Well, you're wrong.

Some places don't get straightened, and some don't get smoothed."

Ashley advanced on us so frighteningly that we pulled together, and virtually hid behind the counter—but she didn't have assault in mind. She was making herself an omelet.

Mom and I nearly laughed with hysteria.

Ashley beat three eggs violently and began chopping peppers and onion. The knife came down frighteningly close to her fingertips.

This is my life, I thought. I'm living here. I, who ought to be worrying about eye makeup and Anthony, college and ski weekends.

Jeffrey's horn blared.

Ash was so startled the knife slipped and she did cut herself. It wasn't much of a cut. A Band-Aid was enough.

But it scared me.

Truly, we were on the edge of violence.

Ashley had cut herself.

But she would rather have cut us.

NINE

Ashley had been home nine days. We Halls were all roughly nine years older.

In carpool Emily said smugly, "I have a truly brilliant advertising campaign worked up. You got your game plan ready, Beethoven?"

Her voice was amused. She did not believe for one minute that I would be able to come up with a game plan. "Certainly. And call me Susan. I'm tired of Beethoven."

"It suits you, though," said Emily.

"It does not. Do I look like an overweight deaf musical genius?"

"Well . . ." said Emily, and we all laughed.

"However," she continued, "I think you should know that Shepherd is a little worried."

"About what?"

"The music section of the yearbook. It would be a

shame to have anything ordinary amidst all the creativity that seems to be coming forth from all the other sub-editors!"

"What makes you think it won't come forth from me too?" I demanded. So the rest of the staff was talking behind my back! Shepherd had chosen me for the focus of her gossip. Saying to them, "I'm afraid Beethoven won't know how to handle an assignment of such magnitude." Saying, "For once I showed poor judgment, didn't I?" And the rest of them agreeing: "Beethoven won't produce. At least, nothing to rival what *we're* producing."

I gripped my books. Their hard ridges bit into my palms.

"But don't worry," said Emily. "Shepherd has some backup ideas in case you don't have anything by Monday."

"Faith," said Swan to me, "don't you love it? The way everyone in this town backs a person up."

I made a face.

"I, Halsey Dexter," he said, "I have faith in you, Susan."

"*Halsey?*" repeated Emily incredulously. "Oh, no. Independence is catching. Beethoven has to be Susan and Swan has to be Halsey."

"Are there any cliffs around here?" said Swan to me.

"I don't know of any. Why?"

"I have this overpowering desire to throw Emily off of one."

"I know the very spot," said Jeffrey gloatingly.

"Jeffrey, I thought you were on my team," complained Emily.

"You backbite too much," said Jeffrey. "Nobody is on your team."

Emily sank back. We had finally hurt her. I thought it would feel good, but it didn't. I really think being a nice person is a terrible burden. You can never enjoy revenge. You just feel guilty.

Sw—Halsey and I exchanged guilty looks. Jeffrey— was this proof of his not being a nice person?—continued to give driving instructions for how to get to the cliff he had in mind.

And there, striding toward the side entrance of the high school, his head ducked against a fierce wind, was Whit Moroso. Long legs in jeans with unlaced high-ankle sneakers, the usual two or three shirts, with a vest lined in fleece. The vest flapped in the wind. Whit was carrying one thin book. How could he do that, and still get the B average I got? I always carried ten fat books, and Whit managed to get through life on one thin one.

He was so handsome.

So dark and inexplicable and expressionless. Did he cultivate that blank look or had he had it from kindergarten? Would it disappear if I got to know him better? Would I be able to see all kinds of things in the slightest crinkle of the eye or quiver of the lips?

But my only chance to get to know him better I had ruined myself.

It was Friday. Game Plan Day was Monday.

I had to approach Whit today, or it would be too late.

Because the trouble with my record idea was—I didn't have the foggiest idea how to begin on it. I could have asked Ashley, of course, whose world was cutting records. But what would be a simple query in another family could be suicidal in mine. So Whit was my only source.

It was nice that my only source was so handsome and so nice and so mysterious.

Sw—Halsey followed my gaze, I supposed because it lasted so long and involved twisting all the way around in my seat as Jeffrey turned right into the parking lot and Whit walked left into the school. "Jeez, Susan," he said softly. "I mean, follow up on Anthony. Don't go falling for some druggie."

"He's not a druggie," I snapped. But very softly, so Emily wouldn't hear.

Emily heard. "Who?" she said. "Who are we talking about?"

"Nobody," I said.

"Tell me, Swan," said Emily.

"I can't be bothered with people who call me Swan," said Halsey.

Another honorable man! I loved it. I leaned over the seat and hugged him, and he grinned, and I said, "You should gave gotten your braces off years ago, Halsey, it's done wonders for you."

"Yeah," he said. "Yeah, yeah." But he liked it.

Trig passed in its usual frightening way, with me having a dim sense of what might be going on, but not a sufficiently strong sense actually to do any of the problems.

I had no chance to speak to Whit and when I looked his way he never looked mine.

In Brit lit, we abandoned Chaucer and were steaming toward Shakespeare. Whit sitting silently behind me was almost more than I could bear. Even when I turned in my seat he didn't look my way, and I was only inches from him. It's a real skill to look casual about ignoring somebody that close.

But I took the egotistical way out. I said to myself, He must like me. Otherwise he wouldn't *care* enough to pretend I'm not here.

All I can see is our bodies entwined,
Both our lives entirely redesigned.

I spent Brit lit trying different versions of that in my journal.

When the bell rang I was the only one not poised for the dash. Nothing at our school is sweet, and bells are no exception: raucous, violent, like something in prisons. Two thousand of us leaped simultaneously out of chairs, which scraped the linoleum on dozens of classroom floors, and began yelling and flinging locker doors open and singing our favorite rock songs and turning on the ghetto blasters for the three minutes of precious passing period freedom.

Except me. I slammed my journal shut, slipped it between two other books, gathered my junk and yelled, "Whit!"

He kept going.

I slithered between the desks and leaped for him, catching a scrap of fabric between my fingers. Rough thick wool. Whit stopped to see what he'd caught his shirt on and saw me down there. He said nothing. He simply looked at the place where I was pulling his shirt out of shape, as though this might be *my* idea of a joke, but it was *his* idea of stupid and I'd better let go. Now.

"Hi," I said.

"I have a class in sixty seconds, Susan."

"I'll be quick," I promised. "Incredibly succinct. A model of brevity."

"Yeah? No sign of it yet."

He did not seem to be joking. Courage and conviction seeped out of me. I glanced around to be sure no yearbook staffers were in earshot. Already the next class was filtering in; Whit and I were blocking the road. "I've thought of my yearbook idea, Whit."

He shrugged, removed my fingers and walked out of the room. I trotted along like an unwanted mutt. How broad-shouldered he was. The shirts barely stretched across the solid muscle of his back. "I need your help, Whit. Please? Would you spend a little while with me after school? I won't—I won't fall apart on you like I did before. I promise."

Whit stopped walking and looked skeptically down at me. As one remembering his mother's lectures on good manners, he said, "What's the idea?"

He has no more faith in me than Shepherd, or Emily, or Jeffrey, I thought, and my face burned with embarrassment. Looking away from him, feeling supremely stupid, caught between my crush and the yearbook, I said, "We could cut a record. Record each rock group, the marching band, the concert choir, and the Madrigals. Bind a slip pocket into the yearbook to hold it. We'd be the only yearbook in the nation with a record in it."

Whit frowned.

Embarrassment had the effect of making it impossible to look at him anymore. I dropped my chin and stared at the linoleum. If things progressed along their usual route, I would now start to cry.

Great.

Half the Wet Duet performs again in public.

"Susan," said Whit, "that's a fantastic idea." He took both my shoulders and shook me a little, excited. A grin spread across his face. It went right into me, like an electrical charge of friendship. Cindy was right. Whit had potential.

"'Course," he added, frowning again, "it would be expensive. But then, this is a rich town. People can afford an expensive yearbook. And if Emily's all she's cracked up to be, the advertising will carry it anyhow."

"Then you'll help me?" I said.

He nodded. "Person you have to talk to is Luce. He and Carmine have been looking into making their own record. They want to stay in rock music."

"You mean you don't?" I said.

"Nah. I don't care about the band."

I couldn't believe it. He had had a taste of success and he didn't want to follow through?

Whit grinned. From the way he smiled down at me I actually thought he was going to kiss me, and I had time to think that yes, I wanted that, and yes, he was worth kissing—but he rocked back on his heels. "Some people want an audience," he said. "I guess your sister was like that. That's what she wanted for her birthday and for Christmas and everything else. An audience."

I stared at him. It explained so much! It wasn't just fame that Ashley craved, it was the audience itself: people applauding her performances. Even an audience of three—us, her family—meant somebody watching her. She didn't care if they liked it. They just had to watch.

I suddenly understood one reason why my parents blocked her way. They didn't think she ought to have an audience. A sweet girl doesn't take center stage. It wasn't the electric guitar or the wild dancing they objected to—it was their daughter before an audience.

But why not? I thought. What's wrong with it? Why couldn't she have that? Out loud I said, "Why don't you want an audience, Whit?"

"I did at first. Then I found out that listening is more fun than performing. Plus, I like money. I'm going into construction with my father. Rock music is no way to earn a living." He laughed. "I guess I don't have to tell Ashley's sister that."

I'm Ashley's sister, I thought. Not Susan. I want an audience too, I guess. People who applaud *me*, not lose their thoughts to my sister. "You do think the record's a good idea then?" I said.

"Yes. And remember what I said about Shepherd. Don't let her know about this. You and I will meet Carmine and Luce to get a few details. Check with the record company they're dealing with. Prices. Numbers. You need a real report for the yearbook meeting. Neat little folders and columns and stuff. That's Shepherd's kind of thing. But don't tell a single other person about your idea. Shepherd would love to do you in."

"I'm not sure why," I said.

Whit laughed. "Sure you are. Sweet suave Anthony glanced in your direction and successful sultry Shepherd can't stand it."

I began to laugh. It was so neat to think that Whit had watched, and understood, and cared.

"Keep laughing, kid," said Whit. "Beats all those tears you keep shedding."

"I'm sorry about the other day."

"Don't worry about it. After you left we talked. I

mean, it's natural your nerves are on edge. Look at all the stress you're under."

Whit, Carmine, Tommy, and Luce understood—while Cindy, Anthony, Jeffrey, Emily, and Shepherd had no concept at all?

The bell rang. Passing period was over. We would both be late to class. As crimes go, it's not much of one. And after Ashley, I have a lot more perspective on minor versus major crimes!

Whit gave me a totally unexpected hug and turned and ran down the hall to his next class.

I stared after him. I could feel the hug pressure from arms that were very strong, from a person enough taller that he had to bend to hug. I should hug more often, I thought, or better yet, *be* hugged more often.

Shivers of pleasure ran over me. I could hardly wait for school to be over so I could join Whit in the band room.

When the final bell rang, I had already decided that Whit and I would go together. I had planned out several dates, and several substitutes in case he had different ideas. I was thinking of my clothes and decided that dating Whit called for an entire new wardrobe. One, preferably, that could be kept hidden from Ashley.

Whit was not there.

Carmine was.

Hulking, stupid, unwholesome. Acne growing on his face like fungus.

I didn't walk all the way into the band room.

"Hi, Susan!" said Carmine eagerly, waving at me. A little boy's gesture in a big man's body. "Whit told me. Great idea. You're really clever, you know? Whit said you were, but I didn't believe him."

Another ego boost. Carmine had had to be argued into thinking I could be clever. Carmine, who probably couldn't even *spell* clever.

I walked closer. This was, after all, the boy who had made up the melody—a very good melody, too—when we composed to my poem.

"We're going over to Ransom Recordings and Printings. They do like you know any kind of reproducing at all, you know? Books and papers and letters and records and tapes and you name it, you know?"

"Sounds perfect," I told him.

He beamed. "I called Mr. Ransom. We have an appointment and everything." Carmine looked surprised by this. "I didn't think he could fit us in on such short notice," Carmine confided, "and a Friday afternoon, and all, but Mr. Ransom said it was no problem."

Carmine did not know that nobody would dare be busy when Carmine wanted to drop by.

Carmine took my arm and led me to the door. "Is Whit coming?" I said nervously. "Nope," said Carmine. "He wanted to, but he hadda make up a test or something. Said to say hi and keep it a secret."

Should I go? If there was any type that your mother warns you against, it's Carmine's type. Especially my mother. "Why is he so sure it needs to be a secret?" I said.

"He don't like Shepherd Grenville. But then, who does?"

In my crowd nearly everybody liked Shepherd. I was not sure who made up Carmine's crowd. One of the good things about a high school this size is you can just avoid the thousand or so kids you think are rotten.

Carmine led me to a car that was an equivalent of the one in which Ashley arrived home. I prayed that nobody I knew would see me in it. I could just hear Emily, laughing gales of laughter for the rest of the carpool year. *Beethoven loves Carmine*—in catchy singsong. And if my mother ever saw us, she would have cardiac arrest. Bad enough that daughter number one had fallen down the sewer—here went daughter number two.

I shifted uneasily on the seat. The upholstery was very torn. I kept feeling as if little rodents probably had burrowed into the openings.

Oh, well, this was Whit's friend. I trusted Whit. He had been kind to me, said nice things, was helping me. Carmine fell into the category of calculated risk.

Mr. Ransom of Ransom Recordings and Printings was a tiny man, about Ashley's size and weight. Carmine towered over him, but to my astonishment, they were old buddies. They laughed, greeting each other, and sort of punched each other and did this little dance of greeting that involved fists and footwork.

I really do think that men are very strange.

Mr. Ransom immediately shoved a chair beneath the backs of my knees, so that I had to sit down or topple. Carmine perched on his huge messy wooden desk, shoving papers out of the way, and playing with the sharp point of a spindle.

"Now the cost per unit," said Mr. Ransom, "no, dear, don't write this down, I'll give you a sheet on it."

He flung open a file drawer—the room was lined with anonymous unlabeled file drawers—and threw a piece of paper at me. Being paper, it just fell to the ground. Carmine loped across the room like a puppy to retrieve it, stabbed it with the spindle and brought it to me with a flourish.

"Now the way we record," said Mr. Ransom, "no dear, don't write this down, I'll give you a sheet on it."

He talked with the speed of a typing class dictation record, but he interrupted himself every line or two to insist that I should not write anything down. Clearly on slow days he entertained himself by drawing up fact sheets. Carmine was kept busy retrieving. Eventually Mr. Ransom tired of this method of communicating with me and began making paper airplanes of his fact sheets.

I grabbed the one that almost flew by my ear. "But we can do it, right?" I said. "My idea is possible?"

"Possible? My dear, it's brilliant. Of course you can do it. All it takes is money."

Well, I would let Emily worry about that. Anyhow, Shepherd had just asked for innovative and unusual ideas; she hadn't said they had to come cheap.

The next paper airplane sailed way above my head, and in spite of a valiant leap Carmine missed it too. It sailed on into the receptionist's office. She hardly missed a beat typing, but merely hurled it right back.

"I would like to work here," I said to Mr. Ransom. "This is my kind of place."

"You would, my dear? No money in it, my dear. Hustle, hustle, hustle, that's the name of this game. Long hours, low income. But it's fun, the way I do it. I think life should be fun. I mean, who needs it if it's not fun, you know what I mean?"

I knew what he meant.

"Now you give me a call, dear, when you know what you're doing. These figures aren't precise. I could do a little better for the high school. Went there myself, you know. Thirty-nine years ago. Isn't that astonishing? Got my fortieth reunion coming up. May as well impress their socks off, you know. Show 'em the Yearbook of the Century. Our yearbook was probably the most ordinary one of the century. We could make a display, my dear, what do you think of that? Like a seesaw. You can be up. I'll be down."

He laughed hugely, reached up to give me a hug, did the same dance in reverse with Carmine, and out we went.

"I adored him," I told Carmine.

"Yeah. Me too. Lotta people you meet in this world, you know, they think they're like royalty or something. He's good stuff, Mr. Ransom. I'd like to work there, too. He told me to go in the Marines for four years first."

"Why?"

"He says they'll straighten me out. I'm not sure I want to get that straight, you know what I mean?"

We drove along like old buddies, cemented by the record idea, by both of us liking Mr. Ransom so much.

I'm something like royalty myself, I thought. A real snob. I wouldn't look at Carmine or at Whit or the rest of Crude Oil as anything but scum. I never gave them a chance. I bet when they made lists of snob princesses, I was right up there with Shepherd and Emily.

But no more.

I sat happily staring out the window. I was a good person. A friend to all. No barriers.

And then I saw that we were just one mile from Iron Mine Road.

My mother could not see me in this car. A boy with a volcanic complexion? In this dreadful car?

All day she would have been coping with Ashley and maybe Bob. She would pass out if I drove up with Carmine. "Carmine, just drop me at the corner, okay?" I said nervously.

"The corner of Iron Mine?" he said. "But it's another mile to your house, Susan, and that's not a good road for walking. No shoulder. The stone walls are right on the edge of the road. I don't mind taking you home."

"No, really," I said, reaching for the door handle. "I love to walk. This is fine. Stop right here."

Carmine stopped very fast. "At your service," he said in a hostile voice.

I licked my lips, trying to think of a way to explain this. Some reasonable excuse. *You look depraved, Carmine. You look like a rock star druggie and my mother can't handle it if you chauffeur me around.*

"I'll have to tell Whit," said Carmine. "He thinks you're a cut above your crowd. But you're just like Shepherd. So get out."

"Carmine, it's not the way it looks. It's—it's—"

"Get outta my car."

I got out of the car.

Boys don't cry. Carmine wasn't crying.

But I had stabbed him.

TEN

Alone.

I needed to be alone badly. I could feel my bedroom waiting for me: soft and quiet, removed from—

But it was not removed.

It had Ashley in it. And black satanic torn tape instead of gentle embroidery.

I wanted to sob for hours, and beat the mattress with my fists and pretend none of it had happened. Or pretend I was brave enough to make a phone call to Whit and explain, and pretend that he was kind enough to understand and talk about it.

But when I dragged up to the front door—what with having to jump out of the way of every approaching car, and then try to miss the stone walls and the poison ivy, it was a long long walk—I was too tired even to go upstairs to my own room. I dumped my books on the hall table and slouched into the kitchen. I felt like something in a compost pile. Rotting at the bottom.

But what a wonderful smell in the kitchen! Warm and good and welcoming. Fresh bread. My mother had been baking. Four loaves of piping hot bread sat on the counter: two dark and crusty, two light and buttery. Mom and Dad were leaning against the cabinets, eating slices just cut from the hottest loaf. Hot bread doesn't cut well, so their slices were thick and shapeless. Slathered with butter. It was like a peace offering.

I didn't bother with a knife, and just ripped a hunk off the same end and chewed. Heaven.

Ashley regarded us all in disgust. We didn't ask her what was disgusting. We just ate on.

"There's soup, too," said my mother. "But maybe we should at least sit down to eat that."

"Mmmmmm. What kind?" said my father through a mouthful of crust.

"Split pea and hambone."

I leaned over the huge copper pot. Everything looks better in the right container. This pot was made for pea soup. The soup was thick, dotted with slivers of ham and flecks of onion. We could hardly bear to waste time setting the table, and sat down without ceremony to spoon in soup and rip off more bread while it still steamed.

Ashley ate nothing.

"What's the matter, dear?" said my mother.

"That isn't even food," said Ashley. "What kind of people get their jollies from vomit green soup and plain bread? Why aren't we having *food*? Lamb chops or steak or something. Something edible."

Very carefully my father set his spoon down. Very carefully he wiped his mouth with his napkin and very carefully he hung on to the side of the table before he addressed Ashley. "When you are earning your own income," he said, "and when you have your own kitchen, you may provide your own lamb chops. Until then, eat what's served and like it."

"Heil Hitler," said Ashley. She began sawing at the other loaf of bread: the crustier, darker bread, which had cooled enough to be easy to cut. Cutting was something to do and she enjoyed it, slowly producing slice after slice. They fell like dominoes onto the tablecloth.

Ashley said, "*Susan* doesn't have to earn a living. *Susan* gets to eat what *she* wants. *Susan*—"

"Is still in high school," said my father. "You will recall that it was your choice to leave school and your childhood behind. Now at twenty-five you suddenly want to be treated like that teenager again? Forget it, Ashley. You're an adult. Start behaving like one."

"Country preacher," she accused him hotly. She made country preacher and Adolf Hitler sound equally horrible. I wanted to laugh. Except that she meant it. She was furious with Dad, and she really thought he was a Hitler, and a country preacher.

"You have to do something productive," said my father, waving the spoon, and in my eyes the spoon turned into a hymn book and I thought, She's right. Once he gets launched on a sermon there's no stopping him until he's rammed the moral home. I wanted to whisper that to Ashley; I wanted to be sisters, friends, share a joke together.

"It's bad for you to hang around," said my father sternly. "Idleness breeds trouble, always has, always will."

But Ashley never left other people space to reach her.

She never looked to any of us for a response, and there was never a way to fit one in. It came to me that she was a remarkably isolated person: All the normal responses—waiting for other people to speak, or smile, or frown in sympathy—all of them were nonexistent in Ashley.

"Productive!" yelled Ashley, slamming her fist on the table. My soup sloshed onto the cloth and the candles trembled in their silver bases. "Listen!" she screamed. "If you'd given me more lessons in—"

My father slammed *his* fist on the table. The salt and pepper jumped. "We gave you everything, Ashley! You have to blame your failure on everything else, don't you? Bad weather kept away your fans. A bad president ruined the economy and contributed to the bad weather that kept away the fans. The fans are stupid. The record stores don't stock the right things. The disc jockeys only play the people who are already established, huh, Ashley? But never never never once did you consider that you were offering a product that wasn't right, did you?"

My mother was shaking. She hates confrontations.

For once Ashley was stung. She looked away and said almost quietly, "I considered that a lot. That's why I changed so often. Trying to hit it right. It's harder than it looks. Getting the combination people seem to want." Her voice broke. For a moment she was vulnerable. Young and scared and terribly terribly sad.

My father said softly, "Sweetheart, you'd feel so much better if you were doing something all day instead of hanging around."

The screams came back full force. "What do you want me to do?" she shrieked, her voice high and bitter and raging. "Sell hamburgers at Burger King? Type invoices at Bloomingdales?" She was gesturing with the bread knife now.

My mother drew back from the table, mesmerized by the swings of that knife. Her fingers knotted around each other like crochet of the flesh.

Ashley spat out, "I am not common! I will not do common things!"

"Oh, come off it, Ashley," I snapped. "You're not a peacock on acid, strutting in front of your fans. We're your mother and your father and your sister and we're not impressed."

The knife flew in front of my face.

There was time to think of being scarred.

Of having my face ruined.

I jerked back, my hand going to my cheek to feel for blood.

But there was no pain.

A lock of my hair, a tiny sliver of brown curl, drifted through a sunbeam, and fell casually to the table.

It was Ashley who retreated to the bedroom.

And that meant I could not go there. I was stranded in the kitchen.

Mom and I did the dishes by hand. We have a dishwasher, but by tacit consent, we accepted hand-washing as a way to work off the pain of that last fight. We actually stood there talking about lemon-scented detergents. "I didn't know real people talked like this," I said to my mother.

"When the alternative is talking about Ashley, real people will seize on anything," she said wryly. "Even lemon-scented detergents."

I waited for her to say, "Susan, you've had enough. A sister who actually uses a knife on you, as opposed to using it on the fan belt, that's too much. She goes. Whether it means the gutter, the police, or what, Ash goes."

But she didn't say that.

My father didn't either.

Mother cleared the table, sweeping that lock of my hair into the garbage along with the used napkins and the spilled food.

We washed. We dried. We put away.

Dishes clinked. Glasses sparkled.

This must have been what it was like in Germany in the 1930s, I thought. Evil all around you, but you don't admit it. You tell yourself you're exaggerating. You put it aside. You tell yourself things will be better in the morning. You do dishes. When you should be running like hell.

Mother vanished into the dining room. When she came back she was dusty and oddly happy-looking. I could not imagine what she could have done in those few seconds to make herself happy.

She brought out the old photograph albums.

The ones from before I was even born.

Ashley, age four, dressed for Sunday school. Little white gloves and little shiny black shoes.

Ashley, age five, playing with a new dollhouse.

Ashley, age six, decorating Valentines.

The present was so dreadful we weren't going to have it around. We were going to reintroduce the past instead. I looked at my mother and thought, Next time you go to the doctor it's probably going to be a psychiatrist.

"She was a lovely little girl," said my mother.

Nobody said anything.

"Wasn't she, Warren?" insisted my mother.

"Yes, Janey," he said, sighing. "A lovely little girl."

On that page, Ashley was making the Valentines and she had gotten sparkle and glue all over her face instead of on the red construction paper. It was one of the most charming photographs I had ever seen.

But that was twenty years ago, I thought. She isn't charming. She's crazy. She took a knife and—

I stopped thinking about it too. It *was* too terrible to think about. I accepted the decision. We would live with Ashley hour by hour, day by day, struggling to make things better, and maybe things really would get better. She was their daughter, she was my sister, and we were not going to give up this time.

I had a rush of love for my parents: for their survival, their sense of humor, their loyalty against all odds. Once again I had to write in my journal. A love song. Not for Whit, not for Anthony, but for families. For solidarity against pain.

I set down the last dish and went into the hall to rummage through my schoolbooks for the journal. I didn't have any words yet, just emotions. Usually the words came first. This would be a different kind of writing: first the thought, then the—

The journal was not there.

At first I couldn't believe it. I must have slipped it into a textbook or between the pages of another notebook. But I flipped pages, and lifted each book, and did it again, and triple-checked.

And it was not there.

I sat weakly on the hall chair: a purely decorative fragile little thing with no function except to fill the corner. In
my whole life I had never sat on it.

Where was the journal?

Where had I lost it?

In Carmine's car? Would he read from it: read it aloud
to Whit when he phoned with the news of what scum I
really was? Would they have a good laugh over it?

Was it on the floor of the music room? In the halls? In
the girls' lav on the second floor? In Miss Margolis'
room?

Who had it? Who was reading it?

I could not bear it if somebody read my journal. I kept
shutting my mind down. I could see Carmine or Whit or
Jeffrey or Emily or Shepherd finding it—but I could not
bring myself to think of them reading it.

It contained the agony of Ashley. The crush on Whit.
The adoration for Anthony. The jealousy toward and
from Shepherd.

The trespass.

But it was my own fault.

I had written it down. Nothing should ever be written
down. Because then it's trapped, and other people can
grab it, and use it, and hurt you with it.

I cried myself to sleep.

Ashley didn't pay any attention.

She was crying herself to sleep too.

ELEVEN

Saturday was a big football game.

Our town is best in swimming, gymnastics, lacrosse and other preppy things. Basketball we haven't won in three years—but then, basketball isn't preppy. You sweat too much in basketball. It's a blue-collar–type game. Football now, that's halfway between. Your preps can sit in the bleachers wrapped in their plaid blankets and have picnics on the tailgates of their cars. So we hang in there in football.

Dad is not our coach. He coaches in New Canaan, one of our big rivals. Today we played New Canaan.

Normally Mom and I won't go to those games, because it's too tough rooting. If we root for us, we're against Dad. If we root for Dad, we're against my classmates. So we don't go.

Today we went. Staying at home with Ashley was more than we could bear.

Just as we had the sit-upons in the car, the sandwiches in the carrier, and the extra blankets folded, Ashley appeared. "I'm coming," she said, which was hardly good news. She was wearing my mother's oldest coat, a huge tweed cloth thing nobody had worn in years. It smelled of a decade of mothballs.

We were unable to restrain our sighs. Was there no rest from Ash?

"You can frisk me for weapons," she said sarcastically.

"Nah. I've brought a gag. That's all we need," I told her.

I thought, somebody at this game has my journal. Somebody there has read my soul, and they're going to walk up to me and there's going to be this knowing glint in their eyes, and I'm going to hate them and myself forever.

And Whit? Would he be there? Would Carmine have said to him, *she's a snobby princess just like Shepherd?* Would he look at me in scorn and contempt?

But no, he would not be there. Weekends he worked with his father. Construction. Masonry: foundations and walls and chimneys. It was hard heavy work and something I would want to do only on sunny breezy blue-skied days. Forget winters, rain, and August.

But that was probably the least of my worries. The real one was: how would Ashley behave? She had not been in public with us before. There was no telling what she might do. Just looking at her secretive face made me cringe. What did she have planned? What terrible revenge would she take on us? She, who had no shame, no pride, no nothing but the desire to shock.

Don't do something hideous, I thought at her.

I even considered begging her to behave. But that would be like inciting a riot. Of course if we had to ask her not to, it would be a matter of honor for Ashley to do something particularly awful.

It was quite cold. The wind was brisk and the bleachers unpleasantly exposed. There was no sun. The sky had the heavy grayness that felt like snow, although it was too early in the year and not cold enough. I told myself at least Ashley, huddled in my mother's coat, would not be stripping and doing some dance in the nude, because she was too cold.

Perhaps she really did want to see the football game.

Perhaps she was actually thinking about some of the things my father had said to her, and planning job interviews and—

Yeah, and Shepherd wanted Anthony to go steady with me, too.

I was just thinking of Anthony when he appeared. It was so dramatic it was like summoning him with ESP. I stared at him. He climbed up the bleachers and sat in the space Ashley had carefully left between herself and me. "Hi, there," he said happily.

"Hi, Anthony. How are you?"

"Fine. Hi, Mrs. Hall."

"Hello, Anthony dear."

My mother adores Anthony. All mothers adore Anthony. No matter what they say about not wanting their little girls to date, or grow up, or go steady or any of that—all mothers want their daughter to go out with Anthony.

Anthony turned expectantly toward the girl sitting on his left. What was I supposed to do? Pretend we weren't related? Pretend she was just a hallucination on Anthony's part? "This is my sister," I said drearily. "Ashley."

"Oh, I'm really glad to meet you," said Anthony, giving her his right hand. "I've heard a lot about you and of course I saw your show when you came to town a few years ago. You were fantastic."

Pride and pleasure crossed her face. I had known Anthony had a way with girls, but I had not known it bordered on the godlike. To win my sister over? Wow.

For the first time we heard anecdotes from Ashley. She sat happily with Anthony, chatting away about this concert and that, this partner and that singer. People she had known, places she had been.

Anthony smiled and nodded and said things like, "Wow" and "Say, that was great," and "Ashley, you are something else!" and my sister blossomed like a daffodil in the first heat of spring.

Anthony had understood. We had not. She needed praise, not condemnation. How thick we had all been. How important it had been to us to show Ash our disapproval. We thought we were supporting her, but we had not even tried. Anthony was the first to bother.

I turned to my mother, but she was watching the game. I had forgotten there *was* a game. I glanced at the field and decided not to bother. Anyhow, things were going to get interesting here on the bleachers, because Shepherd Grenville had spotted Anthony.

Shepherd never wastes time. If there's something to be in on, she arrives immediately. She stepped up the crowded bleachers like a ballerina doing the long-awaited solo. When she arrived in front of us, however, there were no seats, and no place for people to squeeze to give her any room. So she crouched, managing some-how to look utterly attractive and demure in the most awkward of positions.

"So this is the infamous Ashley Hall," said Shepherd, smiling a firm smile, as of one eager to meet a colleague. "What a pleasure."

Ashley simply looked at her. She said to me, over Anthony's body, "Who is that person?"

"That person is Shepherd Grenville," I said. And then, because I knew Ashley would say something nasty, and I yearned for it, added, "She's the yearbook editor. She's just full of exciting nifty little ideas about the yearbook, Ashley."

Ashley laughed. How pretty she was! I tended to forget that she was one beautiful woman. "Yearbook. Exciting," said Ashley. "That sounds mutually exclusive to me. No way to put those words together. But then, if a person has nothing better to do, I suppose it fills the time." She proceeded to ignore the crouching, waiting, smiling Shepherd and continued her conversation with Anthony.

I tried to catch her eye. To thank her for responding so well to an obvious cue line.

But she was absorbed by Anthony.

I was surprised at how well they reacted together! Ashley, who obviously badly needed the admiration, and Anthony, who thrived on caressing girls one way or another.

Meanwhile, Shepherd's knee joints were killing her. Pretty soon she was going to have to stand up straight, and there would still be no place to sit down, and we would still ignore her, and she'd look like a fool.

Hate me more than ever, of course.

But she wasn't acting as if she had found the journal, so who cared?

"So," said Shepherd rather loudly, "the staff meeting is on Monday, Beethoven. You have something ready or not?"

"Beethoven?" repeated my sister, distracted. *"Beethoven?"*

I had forgotten that Ash had never heard this nickname.

"Your sister," explained Shepherd.

Ashley stared at me. "You don't have a musical bone in your body."

"That's why we call her Beethoven," agreed Sheppie happily. "Sort of like calling a tall person Shrimp."

"I like it," said Ashley, assessing me as Beethoven. "Ludwig. Beethoven. Maybe that's what I'll call her. *Susan* never did fit. Too dull."

Shepherd loved that. "Well, she isn't terribly exciting," said Shepherd.

Ashley looked at Shepherd.

It was like a test. Would Ashley defend me, or side with Shepherd?

Ashley said, "Nothing in this town is exciting. You have to leave town even to *think* about excitement."

Around us the crowd screamed madly as the New Canaan team carried the ball toward the goal. Ash glanced at the crowd with great loathing, that they would scream over the possession of a piece of leather and not scream for her music.

Shepherd took Anthony's hand to balance by when she got up, and she didn't let go either. "We have to run along," she said cheerily. "See you Monday, Beethoven."

Anthony did not free himself, but went with her. "Great to meet you, Ashley," he said, with a smile that reinforced it.

Ashley smiled at him, a smile our mother or father would have loved to get.

I watched them descend, tapping people on the shoulder, picking their awkward way down, annoying everybody.

My heart pounded as I noticed Whit standing at the north end of the bleachers, leaning against the fence that wrapped the playing field.

I was amazed at the speed of the physical reaction to him. My whole body knew he was there, and equally cringed and yearned.

Every love lyric I had ever heard or written passed through my mind, a blur of crushes, and they all made sense. I could not bear it if Whit Moroso thought I was worthless.

"I'm going to get popcorn," I said.

"Bring me some," said my mother and Ashley simultaneously.

"Okay." Actually I didn't think anybody was selling popcorn, and I didn't have any money with me, but it was a good excuse. I followed the route Shepherd and Anthony had made, annoying everybody even more, hitting knees, little kids, and handbags.

Whit saw me coming and turned away.

I had to chase him.

It seemed to me I now spent all my time either running from or running after Whit Moroso.

You would think the shame of it would have stopped me, but it didn't. I just lugged the shame along as I chased, flushed with humiliation, thinking—*if he has the journal* . . . Thinking—if Carmine convinced him . . .

"Whit!" I yelled.

The racket from the playing field, and the cheerleaders, and the whistling wind, drowned me out.

But he wasn't running and I was and eventually I got to him. He stood there, expressionless as always, waiting for it to be over.

"Whit, did Carmine talk to you?"

"Yeah."

"I need to explain things."

"I'm not interested, Susan."

He had to be interested!

"You don't know what it's like!" I cried, hanging onto him. "My sister is home. Ashley is a terrible person. She's done terrible things. Even our dog is afraid of her. She—"

Suddenly Whit grabbed me, his fingers tight on my jacket. His grip didn't hurt but it frightened me. His eyes were bright with anger. "You think you're the only one with troubles?" he said softly. "You think having a rotten sister is a ticket to being rotten yourself?"

Rotten? Me?

"Last night," I told him, my voice shaking, "Ashley sliced off a lock of my hair with a bread knife. She has a boyfriend who is evil. And when Carmine was driving me home I panicked."

"Oh yeah? Carmine is evil?" he said roughly.

"No, no, no! But I couldn't have my mother see me getting out of his car. She doesn't know he's kind and bright and a great musician. In fact, the more musician he is, the more terrified of him she'd be. She might think I was going to behave like Ashley. Take drugs and sleep around and go to California and—"

"Okay," said Whit. "Okay. Stop. I get the point." He took his hand away. Mine had dropped already. He stepped back to separate himself from me even more. "Don't panic," he said. "It isn't that important."

"It *is* that important!" Whit didn't know he had become the center of my universe. Anything to do with him was important. But he had no further use for me.

He just wanted this scene to end. I remembered then that Whit had not cared for an audience. All those bleachers full of people—Ashley could have them. Whit did not want an audience.

Love me back, Whit, I thought.

But he merely waited for me to pull myself together. Two tears spilled onto my cheeks but I controlled the rest. The bitter wind hurt where the wetness lay. I brushed the skin with the back of my hand. Whit did not comment.

"What do you mean, I'm not the only one with troubles?" I asked him. "Do you have troubles?"

"What a strange thing to say," said Whit. "Nobody's life is easy, Susan. It's silly to think other people are out there having an easy time of it. They're not."

I disagreed with him. Cindy and Emily and Shepherd and Anthony and people like that sailed smoothly through life. I waited for Whit to tell me what his troubles were but he didn't open up. He was thinking of them, though. He looked both older and younger than I had ever seen him. Vulnerable, I thought. As if he hurts inside.

There was no confiding. He did not trust me.

Gently, facing slightly away from me—or perhaps away from the cruel wind—he said, "I'll help you with the record idea. No problem. Now don't overreact,

Susan. Let me know how the meeting with the yearbook staff goes."

"Thank you."

"Great," he answered, but the word didn't mean *great*, or even *okay*; it meant *at last this scene is over*. He walked on, and waved at me without turning to face me.

TWELVE

Sunday we went to church.

We don't go very regularly anymore, the way we did when Ash and I were little. Mostly we go only if my parents are up early, and the Sunday paper is boring, and my father doesn't have eleven hundred projects to tackle in the basement.

Today none of these things applied.

I don't think my parents intended to pray about Ashley, because I think they had tried that over the years, and achieved nothing, and lost interest in that technique.

I think they wanted an hour of relief from her.

An hour to be utterly civilized, and sing familiar hymns and hear familiar prayers and see familiar faces.

Ashley was asleep when we left so she had no opportunity to threaten to join us.

Church was calming.

Perhaps because it was an hour set aside to think of

higher things. Perhaps because our minister is not very interesting, and the sermon lulled me into a calm that was really boredom. Perhaps, when we prayed to be relieved of all anxiety, I was.

But I think it's more the shape of church.

The reliability of it all.

The institution that has been here thousands of years, will be here generations more. My problems are fleeting; its are everlasting.

And more down to earth, when they make a plea for money for the soup kitchen in New Haven, and tell you how many hungry mouths need to be fed during the coming winter, your rotten sister recedes in importance.

So after church we went to the coffee hour and chatted up people we hadn't seen in ages, and took a leisurely drive home, by way of the doughnut place, and decided that afternoon we would take a family drive.

We turned into Iron Mine Road feeling pretty good. I felt I could deal with whoever had found my journal. I felt I could face Whit and Crude Oil without weeping. I felt senior year would go on, and I would be all right, and all trials would pass.

And there were police cars in our driveway.

"Oh, no, please no!" whispered my mother, clutching my father.

My father sucked in his breath and muttered things to himself, or to God, but I couldn't quite hear.

Bob's van was there. The police had Bob propped up against the side of it, legs spread, hands up, frisking him. A bad scene in a bad cop show—only it was our driveway.

Ashley was screaming and yelling, and cops were

holding her, and she was writhing like some sort of little animal, trying to kick their shins.

Neighbors—Mrs. Boyd, the McLeans, everybody—were standing on their porches or in their yards.

Loud, incredibly painfully loud music blared everywhere.

My mother did not even try to get out of the car, but just sat there, her head sunk in her hands. My father leaped out, going to help the policemen hanging on to Ashley.

I could not think of anything but stopping the music. At that level it was not music. It was an assault on every sense; like a battlefield; like guns instead of drums. I turned off the radio in the van, but the blaring went on. I turned off the radio in Dad's pickup truck, but the blaring managed to continue even then. In the house I found the kitchen radio, my bedroom radio, the television, a portable radio, and the radio we never use that's incorporated in the stereo system—all turned up full volume. They were all on the same station except the television, of course, which was screaming out cartoons.

The cessation of rock music was a slap of silence.

It had a sense of familiarity. Crude Oil, I remembered. The pain of Whit washed over me again. I staggered to the front door. My sister was getting arrested and I was thinking of a crush that had gone nowhere.

When I got outside, Mrs. Boyd was comforting my mother. Bob had been put into the backseat of a police car, which could not have been an easy task, given Bob's weight. "He violated parole," said Mrs. Boyd rather happily. "Isn't it a good thing I called the police. That gets rid of *him* for a while."

I looked at my neighbors and realized that they had

suffered along with us. Not wanting to interfere, wanting to let Ashley come back to the fold, wanting to let us be—but frightened of Bob, frightened of Ashley, locking their doors even as we had locked ours.

Ashley was a fountain of bad words, spewing them everywhere, at the police, at my father, at the world.

On the grass near the police car was a black-and-white splotched notebook.

I approached it timidly. I pushed it with my toe to see if it was mine. And it was.

From the backseat of the car Bob laughed evilly. "You thought you had some good stuff in there, didn't you, little girl?" he screamed. "Well, you didn't. We were going to pirate it, but there was nothing worth a nickel in that stupid notebook. A lot of emotional crap. Nothing good."

Bob had read my notebook.

Nausea welled up in me. Dizziness swept over me.

Ashley giggled. A high-pitched crazy little giggle.

My journal.

I felt, to use the crudest terms I knew, truly shit upon.

I would have used tongs to pick up the journal, but there were limits even to my silliness. I leaned over without fainting, picked it up, and took it inside. I stared at it for a long time, and then I opened the kitchen garbage and stuffed it into an empty Rice Krispies box and covered that with used napkins and tied the plastic garbage bag shut.

Outside the police cars drove off.

They took Bob.

They left Ashley.

I thought, that isn't fair. Why didn't they take Ashley?

Why did they give her another chance? Why do we have to take more of this?

I almost crawled up the stairs to my room. I thought: I'll get under the covers where I can't see the walls and I'll be safe under there.

Upstairs, Ashley had turned her bed upside down. Not the mattress but the bed itself. The result, with high pencil posts, was a queer sort of cage, with the mattress stuffed on the floor. Perhaps she was making herself a cave. I squatted down to look inside.

Inside all my stuffed animals were lined up. Teddy, Eeyore, two zebras, a few rag dolls, a heart pillow, Kanga with Roo in her pocket, a Garfield, and a Snoopy. My favorite teddy, dressed like a detective (Bearlock Holmes), sat in front.

I looked closer.

Ashley had brought her bread knife up here.

Their little throats oozed stuffing.

THIRTEEN

"Wayne," said Shepherd, consulting her legal pad, "we'll hear from you first."

She had managed to intimidate all fifty of us. How utterly poised and elegant she looked. You could not imagine Shepherd ever failing. Like the goddess figurehead on a whaling vessel, facing waves of icy water, she would sail on. The rest of us would probably fade at the first high wind.

Wayne was caught by surprise. He glanced across the room, was appalled by the number of faces and spoke from his seat. "No, no, Wayne," said Shepherd. "Come up front where we can all see and hear."

I think Wayne would gladly have been hit by a car rather than stand in front of us, but he obeyed, shuffling up next to Shepherd. "Well, like, I'm doing sports," mumbled Wayne, not looking at anybody. "And like, we thought maybe this time instead of just still photographs of each team, and like a list of like the trophies and stuff they won and all . . ."

He had nothing in his hands. Shepherd had known enough to have legal pads and file folders to hold. She stood there like a teacher, or a jailer, and smiled while Wayne flushed and stumbled his way through his idea. Wayne's a fairly good round-about athlete, on several teams, but a starter on none. I like Wayne. Considering how unnerved he was to be in front of us, he did a good job. Certainly we all knew what he was saying.

Shepherd interrupted gently to summarize for him, as if we could not possibly have grasped his idea. "In other words, Wayne, you are going to have a series of action photographs, so each two-page spread will resemble an actual game in progress."

Wayne nodded. "But like some of the time we had pretty lousy teams."

We all laughed.

Wayne managed half a grin and said, "We can't show the action there because like we don't want to show a score of losing fifty-six to three. Like say the fencing team? This is the first year we've had fencing and we're pretty bad. Sorry, Derek," he said to the lone fencer in the room. Derek just shrugged, smiling. "So like we'll show like the equipment and the expression on the face behind the mask like."

Shepherd said, "Like, well, like I think we like see what you have in mind like, Wayne." Her mimicry was perfect. She made Wayne sound dumb without making herself sound mean. Several people, including Jeffrey and Emily, laughed at Wayne.

I hated her.

Wayne's idea was excellent, and the sports section would be infinitely more memorable the way he was designing it. But she had made him look like a fool.

But then, the more fools she had around her, the more she would shine.

I was suddenly aware of a very strange thing.

My dislike of Shepherd was much stronger than my dislike of Ashley. Somehow Ashley, no matter how rotten she was, wasn't as rotten to my mind as Shepherd. How odd, I thought. Why do I feel that way? Ashley has never given me any hope. Things are worse than ever.

But I would rather deal with Ashley than Shepherd.

Shepherd put the art editor on the spot, but the art editor was much too loose to be bothered. She was your typical free spirit and Shepherd could sail forever and the art editor would never even notice her on the horizon.

Three cheers for the art editor, Penny.

Shepherd's long slender fingers tapped gently on the pale vanilla folders she had marked for each division of the yearbook. Carefully working through them, frowning slightly at each label, she drew out one. My stomach tightened. What would she do to me? She had exposed Wayne like so much hamburger meat. Me she hated.

I looked Anthony's way, which was a mistake, because he looked right back, grinned to me, waved and mouthed, "Talk to you later?"

Unfortunately Shepherd saw this.

She did not look at me. She merely looked down into her folders, as though she had dynamite there and would blast me away.

What if my idea wasn't as good as I thought? Whose

opinion did I have, after all, but Whit's? And nobody in this room was like Whit, and maybe nobody in this room thought like him, either. My idea was very different, very expensive. What if they shot me down? What if they all groaned and said, "Beethoven, be real."

What if they laughed at me, the way some of them had laughed at Wayne?

My hands began to sweat. I wiped them surreptitiously on my jeans. It felt as if the whole room had seen this and analyzed it. Why Beethoven, you're perspiring, are you nervous—naturally you're nervous, because you're stupid, and so is your idea.

"Now the real innovation in the yearbook," said Shepherd, gracefully drawing a folder from her collection, "is letters of congratulation. Letters wishing our graduating class best of luck in the future."

Was she joking? A bunch of letters was supposed to be an innovation?

"I've written to several famous people already," said Shepherd. "So far I have replies from seven of them." Her excitement was genuine. She expected us to be thrilled. We just looked at her oddly.

But then she began reading them aloud.

The people she had written to!

She had letters from the president of the United States, from the premier of Israel, from the mayor of New York City, from a television anchorwoman and a rock star my sister would have died for and from the queen of England!

I could not believe they had answered! Imagine those people taking the time—or telling their secretaries to—and writing to *us*, telling us how proud they were of our accomplishments and how much they expected of us in the decades to come. When she held up the letter from the President, and we saw the letterhead

THE WHITE HOUSE
Washington

it was very very impressive.

Shepherd got a round of applause and she deserved it. Hers was a fantastic idea and it was going to work.

Shepherd pulled out another folder. She smiled into it, and I knew it was mine. MUSIC, it would say, in neat block letters. And as she removed the folder, and turned to face me, and started to call upon me to rise and shine, I saw that the folder was full.

Full?

Full of what?

This was my section, to be filled with my ideas. What could it already be full of?

Emily and Jeffrey had told me Shepherd had backup ideas. They had not been joking. What if her ideas were better than mine? What if she let me speak, turned me down, and then whipped out her *own* brilliant gaudy Harvard-bound idea?

Shepherd looked at me, letting a little time go by, so the whole room could see she was a little dubious about calling on me. Wayne said, "Whatsa matter, Sheppie? Forget what you're doing?" He grinned at me, and I thought, so he knew what was going on too. He was just too nervous to combat it. Well, I had an ally. Wayne.

I stood up. The paper in my hand rattled a little. Shepherd looked at it, cocking her head. I slid past four sets of knees. Wayne muttered, "Give her hell, Beethoven." It did not seem like the right moment to ask Wayne to call me Susan.

"So, Beethoven," began Shepherd. "What do you have in store for us?"

"I'd like to introduce myself," I said to her. "My name is Susan Hall and I'm your music editor." I turned to the rest of them. "This is senior year, guys. I cannot be Beethoven during my senior year. So it's Susan, okay?" I grinned, but it was bravado. I was more scared than Wayne would ever be.

The back door to the meeting room opened.

Nobody turned. Perhaps nobody heard the faint creak. Even Shepherd did not see, because she was reaching into her own music file.

It was Whit.

He slouched in the doorway. He didn't smile at me. He lifted his chin fractionally and winked.

I had a cheering section.

A little on the silent side, to be sure.

But my own.

I said, "Our yearbook will not just have photographs and reproductions of letters. No matter how we arrange photographs, that's all they are—and essentially that's what any yearbook has. Photographs. And after all, music has nothing to do with photographs. A photo of a marching band doesn't tell you a thing except the color of the uniform. A photo of Crude Oil doesn't tell you what their music sounds like. Music is something you have to hear, not see."

They were confused. Shepherd was getting her poise back.

"So we're going to cut a record."

Whit grinned. I had not seen a grin as wide as that since the moment in the electronic music lab. He leaned back against the door jamb and grinned at the ceiling and then back at me, and he was savoring my triumph as much as I was.

"We'll tape the four rock bands that have managed to stick together since we were all sophomores. And the marching band, the concert choir, the Madrigal group. I've spoken to the recording company, I have the figures and the costs. We're going to bind a slip pocket into the yearbooks and every single graduate will have a *real* record of what we did musically."

Jaws fell open.

Eyes widened.

Whispers began.

Smiles spread on skeptical faces.

I referred to my paper. I gave them the cost per unit, on a sliding scale of how many records we might order. The time involved. The taping schedule. The problems of binding slip jackets into the yearbook. How Crude Oil was going to arrange the actual taping. How—

Anthony was on his feet. In his way, Anthony had more force of personality than Shepherd. When he leaped to his feet, he brought others with him, as if they were bound to his motions. When he clapped they did, and when he stomped his feet, they followed suit. "Way to go!" he shouted, punching the air with his fist like a basketball player who just sank a foul shot. "We really *will* have the finest yearbook in the United States of America."

They swarmed around me, hitting me on the back, hugging me, shouting to each other. Sheppie had told us we would have the finest yearbook in the nation and here was the proof. Beethoven—I mean, Susan, they corrected themselves quickly—had done it.

Shepherd set down her music folder. Quickly, pretending she wasn't, she covered it up with her other folders.

Which meant her backup idea was nothing compared to my idea.

I looked up to catch Whit's eyes and share the victory. He was gone.

I was swamped with volunteers to be on my committee. Somebody handed me a piece of paper and I jotted down names and said I would call them. Derek and Wayne gave me hugs and said they loved me. Shepherd very stiffly congratulated me. I told her how exciting the letter from the president was. Anthony said, "Susan, you want to have a Coke with me?

"Oh, Anthony, I'd love to," I said. And it was true. I would love to. "But I promised my mother I'd be right home. I have to catch the second bus."

"Ugh," said Emily. "All those disgusting sophomores and juniors. People who've had their driver's license twenty-four hours and carry SAT prep guides around with them."

Jeffrey said, "I'll take you home, Susan. Forget the bus."

Wayne said, "Aw come on with us, Susan. Anthony and Derek and I are going over to Dom's with Caitlin and Pammy. Come with us."

Caitlin and Pammy. The two most beautiful popular girls in the class, giving even Shepherd Grenville a run for her money.

I almost said yes.

But my mother had been crying that morning.

Actually she hadn't stopped crying since the night before.

And I had promised to come straight home. Would she understand, if I took an hour to go to Dom's with Wayne and Anthony and Derek and Caitlin and Pammy?

Anthony, sensing hesitation, put an arm around me and snuggled. "Come on," he said. "You know you're dying to." He twined fingers in my hair.

Shepherd stood very still.

Cindy, my best friend, watched. I knew she celebrated for me. If she was envious, it didn't show. She was keeping back so she wouldn't interfere. She knew Wayne and Derek and Anthony and Caitlin and Pammy wouldn't ask her along.

I'm a star, I thought. They want me. I succeeded. It's all in the courage. When I was wimpy and let them call me Beethoven and cringed when Shepherd spoke to me, who needed me? But let me stand up and produce and place demands and I'm attractive.

You don't have to *dress* for a crush, I thought. You have to *show off* for a crush. They like the ones with spunk.

Anthony tugged my hair gently. Cindy grinned, and I knew she was thinking of our conversation about the red and gold of autumn in my hair. "Great," said Anthony. "That's settled. Come on."

"I didn't say yes," I protested.

"Yeah, but you *meant* yes." He started walking with me. I liked it—in fact I loved it—but I wasn't sure. My mother, crying, touching my sweater with her bitten fingertips, a used Kleenex balled in the other hand, whispering, "Susie, don't stay late, I need your company. Please."

"I can't, Anthony. I really can't. My mother needs me.

It's kind of a difficult situation at home right now and I'd love to go with you another day, okay?"

They didn't shrug, make faces, or abandon me. They actually looked impressed. It's Ashley, I thought. They know the difficult situation is Ashley. Ashley adds to my status. I really am a woman of mystery and creativity to them.

"Okay, okay," said Anthony, sighing dramatically. "But I'll drive you home."

If this was stardom, no wonder Ashley strove for it. To be sought after! To have people change their plans for you!

"I just have to go to my locker first," I said.

"Okay. Meet you at the front door." Anthony kissed me goodbye, possessively, as if we were already going together.

I wasn't sure what to think of that. But I left the room quickly. I didn't go to my locker. I had all the things I needed. I ran down two flights and up one long dark hall to the electronic music lab.

Locked and dark.

The band room.

A brass group was rehearsing there. The band leader looked up irritably when I swung the door open. "Sorry," I muttered.

The choral room.

Empty.

Rows of metal folding chairs arranged for the concert choir sat in dim silence.

No Whit.

I walked to the front door. Anthony was waiting for me, smiling.

Anthony talks easily, I had learned that much. I didn't need to contribute much to encourage him. "Last time I drove you home, you abandoned me so fast I hardly saw the dust from your shoes," he teased. "Do I get to come in this time?"

Oh *why* couldn't I have a normal family life like everybody else? Like my own, until Ashley descended upon us? I said hesitantly, "I'd be glad to have you come in, but my mother's in kind of rough shape. She might have a hard time with company."

"You," said Anthony, "are riding with the most sensitive guy in town. I get one flicker of feeling that your mother doesn't want me around and pffft! I vanish into the night. Promise."

I giggled. "It wouldn't be you personally," I explained. "She might be tense or upset and would only want family around." Actually she might not be too thrilled about having one member of the family around either, but I wouldn't explain that much.

"Trust me," said Anthony, and I trusted him.

My mother was at the kitchen table. Fingers fastened to a mug, but no steam rising. From the way she sat, I thought the tea had been cold for hours. "Hi, Mom." I bent to kiss her. "Anthony Fielding came home with me. How about I make you another cup of tea?" She didn't look that bad, really. She had been doing more thinking than weeping.

"Hello, Anthony," she said, smiling at him. He gave her a swift hug, which astonished me until she said, "You've certainly grown since you were a Cub Scout in my troop."

"You still the volunteer of the decade?" said Anthony, sitting beside her and handing me her cold mug. He gave her a quick Cub Scout salute.

She beamed. What ability Anthony had to recognize people the way they wanted to be recognized! She talked a little about this year's volunteer work, and Anthony told her he was doing quite a bit of sailing, but he was into racing now more than cruising and he was trying to talk his father into getting him a new boat.

I got Cokes for the two of us and stood over the stove waiting for the water to boil for Mom's tea. They didn't need me in the conversation. I felt very happy. The kitchen was the place where I had lived for years: untouched by Ashley, filled with friends and contentment. I poured the tea and let it steep.

"Thank you, darling," said my mother, getting up. "I have some phone calls to make. I'll do them from the bedroom." She smiled at Anthony. "Flower Committee at church. I knew I shouldn't have gone yesterday. They roped me into it. I couldn't refuse."

"Sure you could have," he told her. "My mother is a terrific refuser. Saying no is what she does best."

"Mom doesn't want to say no," I explained. "Or she would, too." I didn't want Anthony to think she was a wimp people pushed around. And right up until she winked at me I thought she really did have phone calls for the Flower Committee. Then I figured out that a girl who brings Anthony Fielding home is a girl who deserves a little time alone with him.

Anthony switched from sailing to skiing. "We have a nice little condo in northern Vermont," he said.

I was willing to believe it was in northern Vermont, but

it would not be a "nice little" place; it would be a sumptuous big place.

"You ought to come skiing with us," he said. "First snowy weekend we get. How about it?"

I was thrilled. "Anthony!" I breathed. *And part of me thought—but Whit—what about Whit?*

Anthony told me about snowy weekends he had known.

And Ashley came into the room.

We gasped in unison, looked at each other in total astonishment, and looked away to keep from laughing. The only good thing you could say about her clothing was that it wasn't mine.

Canvas drawstring pants. Torn. High-heeled sequined boots. Rose red. Exotic plumed feathers drifting down her shoulders and a blouse that looked as if it had been savaged by a pack of vultures. She had worked perhaps a dozen chains into her hair, fastening them to an almost hidden barrette, and they clanked and glittered.

She looked out of order, lost from a costume party.

It's the house, I thought. You can't dress like that in a house built in 1774. For that outfit, you need a wild, sophisticated stage set and bright lights and a background of throbbing loud music. Wouldn't Whit and Carmine, Tommy and Luce love writing the music for that outfit?

"Like it?" said Ashley anxiously, as if she actually valued our opinion. "Bob and I put it together. Wouldn't it look great on a stage?" Her voice was wistful. "I used to spend so much on costumes. Make a fortune on one tour and blow it all on costumes for the next." She said to Anthony, "You're nothing if you don't look fantastic."

Anthony recovered nicely. "You qualify," he said.

"That is some outfit! And with stage lights focused on it—fantastic."

Ashley beamed and pirouetted, showing off like a child in dancing school. "Once," she confided, "we had neon tubes put in a clear plastic keyboard. In the drumsticks, too, so that when we dimmed the lights, our instruments went neon red, blue, and yellow. Cost megabucks."

She put the radio on. Mom had it tuned to the local station (she likes Swap Shop, the Tidal Calendar and Shoreline Newsline) which merited a glare from Ashley and a quick whiz through the stations back to rock. I didn't know the piece they were playing. Ash began dancing to it: clumping, really. More convulsions of the skin and limbs. Nothing graceful. And yet she looked very effective doing it: charged with electricity. I thought she probably had been very good on stage.

If she hadn't been my sister, I probably would have loved it, too.

Anthony was mesmerized. You Fieldings have four Mercedes, I thought, but you don't have an Ashley. Bet you're jealous, huh?

"You're the one who loved my show," said Ashley.

Anthony was nothing if not gallant. "Yes. I can still remember it so clearly." Every cue line she gave, Anthony responded to. He practically had her purring at his feet. He had told me he was the most sensitive guy in town, but anybody who could figure out the right moves with Ashley Elizabeth Hall went beyond mere sensitivity into mind-reading.

"Wait a second," said Ashley. "I have to get something." She smiled at Anthony excitedly, and clicked speedily up the stairs. By the sound of her steps I knew she was in my parents' room. Now what piece of costuming could she possibly expect to find in my mother's staid tailored wardrobe?

"Life is pretty exciting around here, isn't it?" said Anthony, in what I thought was a classic understatement. I smiled at him and nodded, but I thought exciting was hardly the word to describe it. Anthony kept his eyes on the door through which Ash would return. He was fascinated by her. It must all be very romantic to him. The fallen rock star, come home to lick her wounds. The girl who had been everywhere, done everything, dancing for Anthony Fielding.

"You know, I was really impressed by your idea for the yearbook," he said. "So was everybody. But what I couldn't get over was the picture of you going to Crude Oil for help. That is one tough crowd." He shook his head. "But now I see why it didn't faze you. You probably have that type of guy around all the time, huh?"

I had no idea what to say to him. Did he think Whit and Carmine were like Ashley? Did he think that Ashley was really very sweet under a rough facade? Did he think that Whit was really vicious under an expressionless facade?

But I was spared answering. Ashley came back—cheeks flushed, eyes bright. But it wasn't anything taken by mouth or by vein that had done that: It was the admiration of a handsome boy for her music. "How old are you, Anthony?" she said.

Oh, no. She was going to proposition him.

"Eighteen. I should have graduated in last year's class, but I had to repeat first grade."

"You're kidding."

"Nope. I was a six-year-old dummy. Had a real hard time with the alphabet."

But what she had in her hand was our household's sole copy of her album, which my mother kept among the things like her eighth-grade diploma and her second-grade perfect attendance at Sunday School document. Ashley had really been doing some searching, I thought. And who had done it with her? Bob? Had Ashley and Bob crawled through my parents' things?

We keep the stereo in the dining room because we so rarely walk through there that it's safe from bumps and vibrations. We eat at the kitchen table because of the beautiful view. Ashley danced into the dining room to put her record on.

Conversation was impossible after she turned the volume up to her preferred level, so we sat and listened. Ash slid into a trance of happiness. Even for Anthony I could not take my eyes off her. She was listening to her greatest triumph and most lasting failure. Because this was what she had never duplicated. Success.

We heard the whole side. Most numbers were too harsh for me. They were no longer in style. The whole record had a very dated feel, as if we were dipping back into history. Maybe we were. Maybe Trash was history and the exotic exciting Ashley that Anthony thought he was dealing with really existed.

The music stopped. Ashley opened her eyes and focused on Anthony. Anthony responded as I knew he would. With compliments.

"I like that," he said, smiling into her smile.

And then the guillotine dropped.

Anthony said casually, "Who did it? It was different."

Ashley's brightness dimmed. "Who did it?" she repeated slowly.

"Yeah." Anthony picked up my hand from where it rested on the placemat. My hand was cold. He held it flat between his two palms. "Interesting. A little unpolished compared to what people are doing now, don't you think? But it's nice to listen to the oldies now and then, isn't it?"

Ashley stared at him. Pain and rage fought in her features. I hoped that pain would win and she would creep quietly away and nurse her hurt in private. But with Ashley, temper surfaced before anything.

"You lying, conniving, scummy *shit!*" she screamed, hurling the pottery sugar bowl at him. He jerked back and it caught his shoulder without really hurting him. He stared at me, frozen, willing me to tell him this wasn't happening. Ashley warmed up, calling him the most awful names she knew. Anthony was truly shocked. Ten days ago I would have been too, but now I knew all her awful names. I tried to keep holding his hand, but he was up from the table, standing, just as mesmerized by Ash the Trash as he had been by Ash the Sweet.

"Ashley," I said, trying to calm her, "he just didn't recognize your band. That's all."

"That's all! At the football game he told me how much he loved my group. He told me he remembered my music. He was just making conversation. He was lying." She was spitting the words out at him, like nails from a power driver.

"It's okay to be polite," I said.

Ashley ignored me. Her voice thinned, became evil. She hissed at him *"Get out of this house."*

Anthony looked blank, as if Ashley's curses had

blinded him. "I'm really sorry, Anthony," I said, not taking my eyes off Ashley either. "You'd better leave."

He moved toward the door but not fast enough to suit Ashley. I tripped her. There was nothing else to do. "Mom!" I screamed. "Dad!" She slipped on the spiky heels and hit the sideboard without falling all the way. A candlestick toppled over and she saw it and grabbed it. Twelve inches of solid brass. *"Anthony, get out of here!"* I screamed. *"Ashley, put that down!"*

My sister is democratic. Better to hit the girl you aren't mad at than chase after the vanishing boy you are mad at. But I had the advantage over Anthony. I had seen her try to bite, kick, and rip the cops who had held her. He had really thought she was a sweet person that the community had somehow misunderstood.

He fled.

I ran around the table to get away from Ashley.

My father took the basement steps three at a time. My mother almost fell down the other stairs trying to reach us. It is not fun, treating your sister like a rabid animal.

Whenever we loosened our grip, tempting, since she was kicking with her sharp little boots—she attacked the furniture. She hurled a chair, threw a clock and smashed some china. Finally my father—who in my opinion should have done this days ago—simply took her in a lock position with her arms behind her, twisted so that she could not move without considerable pain.

We stayed that way for a long time: My mother and I staring at Ashley, my father hanging on to her, Ashley's face slowly sagging with exhaustion.

My mother sank into her usual chair. "You're right, Warren," she said dully. "I will stop arguing. We will have her committed."

FOURTEEN

All my life my parents have celebrated triumphs with dinner out at an Italian restaurant called the Open Door. It isn't much to look at, but we love it. It serves the hugest yummiest meals anywhere, in the friendliest atmosphere. If Dad's team unexpectedly manages to beat their strongest rival, or the Vietnamese immigrant Mom is tutoring passes a literacy test, we go to the Open Door.

I had just presented the most brilliant idea ever mentioned in a yearbook committee meeting and gotten a standing ovation.

But we didn't go to the Open Door.

I didn't tell my parents about the yearbook. Not because they wouldn't have listened, but because I had forgotten.

My sister had been home less than two weeks and she already had us at the point of putting her into an institution. To protect us, rather than to help her!

My father said, "The two possibilities are Valley Hospital for the Mentally Ill and Cherry Hill Home for Young Adults."

"It's my fault," said my mother. "The moment Ashley sliced up Susan's sweater and smashed her cassettes we should have gotten rid of her. But I couldn't bear it. To throw out my daughter in less than twenty-four hours? I couldn't bear it." Her eyes were fixed in space. Perhaps she was seeing the Ashley Elizabeth she had always wanted to have: the one who existed now only in photograph albums.

"It's my fault," she said again. "I'm too passive. I was the wrong parent for Ashley. It was easy with Susan. I could say *now, dear,* or *be nice, dear,* or *say you're sorry, dear* and that was all it took with Susan. But Ashley needed" —she stared vacantly at her oldest daughter. She had never known what Ashley needed. Didn't know now.

It is your fault, I agreed silently. You were too passive. And you did give only the things you felt like giving. But what does it matter now? Ash is twenty-five. She is her own responsibility.

I thought of my stuffed animals, their little throats slit. My sweater, dripping yarn. My clothing, mutilated.

What would it be like on Ash's twenty-sixth birthday? Would we visit her in an institution? Would we be in court, trying to keep her locked up where she couldn't hurt us? Or would we be right here, playing the same tune with the same group?

My father eased Ashley into her chair. She didn't struggle. She had run out of energy. She sat, her colored feathers torn and drooping, and the silver and gold chains in her hair matted and broken.

She was a wreck. Like a ship dashed on the rocks.

There is only one good thing, I thought.

She came home.

When everything in the world failed for her, she knew she could come home.

My father tilted back in his chair, telephoning a number he had written on a slip of paper in his wallet. From the half of the conversation we could hear, he was talking to the hospitals about admitting Ashley.

What if I do something bad? I thought.

Or what if life does something bad to me?

Home has to be here.

"Happily ever after," I said out loud.

They looked at me.

"It's my favorite sentence," I said, embarrassed. "I wanted to use it for us. I want things to be happily ever after."

My father cupped his hand over the phone. "Forgiving is easy," he said. "But we have to survive. It's time to cut our losses."

"What am I, a stock investment?" said Ashley.

I like peaceable things. Gentle things. Smooth unruffled things. If Ashley stayed she would defile my bedroom again. But if we threw her out . . .

My father hung up. "Well," he said tiredly, "you get your wish."

He was speaking to all of us.

"Valley has no openings. And Cherry Hill takes only voluntary admissions." He stared hopelessly at his older daughter. "Ashley, would you consider signing yourself in for treatment at Cherry Hill?"

"My sister and mother are willing to give me another chance," said Ashley. "How come you aren't?"

"I guess eight hundred seemed like enough," he said sarcastically.

I didn't like him.

For the first time in my life I looked at my own father and I didn't like him. You can be understanding to every kid who ever played on your football teams, I thought, but you won't try to understand Ashley. She's right. You never did try.

On the other hand, what good was it to understand? The hooked rug was just as ruined, the bedroom just as defiled, and the sweater just as mutilated, whether I understood or not. And he was right, too. Eight hundred times was enough chances.

How do people ever see things clearly? I thought. There are too many angles to everything.

"You're not dating that lightweight preppy idiot, are you, Susan?" said my sister.

"No, Ashley. And thanks to you, I guess I never will be."

Ashley smiled. "My good deed for the day."

School.

Everyone was so excited by my yearbook idea they could hardly see straight. People I hardly knew ran up yelling, "Susan! Great idea!" People in marching band told me their favorite march and people in concert choir wanted to know if they could record *two* songs. A jazz group reminded me that they existed and asked not to be left out. I referred them all to Whit.

Emily told me she knew already that there would be enough sales to make up for the added cost of the record because people were so thrilled.

Anthony never looked my way. He kept his face averted and conversed deeply with other people, especially Shepherd. If I'd had energy to spare for grief, I would have grieved. Anthony, of all people. If Whit had had to deal with Ashley, he'd have grabbed her like my father did and held her down until she surrendered. But Anthony—

He had no way to know how to deal with it.

No more than my mother did.

It was a case where practice meant nothing. You were either able to handle Ashley or you weren't.

We weren't.

In trig, Miss Margolis said, "We're taking a quiz, Susan. Remember? That's why there's a pencil in your hand."

"Oh, is *that* why she's hanging on to the pencil," said Jeffrey. "And here I thought she was going to perform an unnatural act with it."

"That's her sister you're thinking of," said Karen Campagne. "Susan here is Miss Conventional."

"I always thought the name Ashley Hall sounded like a boarding school," said Jeffrey. "You know. The kind where girls have a nine-o'clock curfew and go to chapel on Sundays and all the graduates are just so, so socially acceptable."

"Can't be Ashley. She was *never* socially acceptable."

They were trying to be funny. They thought it was just easygoing kidding. They figured a status type like me (yearbook originator and all that) would have a good laugh.

What would they do if I began screaming? Pounding my fists and hurling my books like Ashley?

"I can always tell when you're having fun," Whit murmured in my ear. "Your knuckles turn white."

His long legs stretched past his own desk to flank mine. All boys have huge feet. I sometimes wonder how they can hoist all that without tripping. I turned to smile at him. He had had a haircut. How handsome he was! Positively preppy. Oh, Whit! I thought. Maybe Ash did do a good deed, getting rid of Anthony for me.

My crush on Whit was so tangible I could have held it in my hands.

But it was not Whit who caught me after class. It was Shepherd. Whit wouldn't hang around when Sheppie was there, so any chance to talk to him vanished. "Susan," she said, taking a deep breath, "my parents recommended calling the newspaper and getting some publicity on the yearbook."

"Yeah?"

"With the focus on your record."

I had truly stolen her thunder. I had to admire her, though. She was admitting that it was my project that deserved the publicity.

"The reporter can talk to us tomorrow fifth period or the following day after school. Can you manage one of those times?" She had to work to put the smile on her face.

Planning as far as tomorrow fifth period was beyond me. After all, I still had to go home tonight, and do normal things like homework while Ash cut the buttons off my shirts.

Cindy materialized at my elbow. I had forgotten I had a best friend. Less than two weeks of Ash and all things near and dear had splintered away. "Can she talk to you later, Shepherd?" said Cindy. "Things are a little unsettled right now."

"Fine," she answered, looking confused.

"Great," said Cindy, leading me away.

"We're going to be late to class," I objected. My lips felt numb, as if I'd gotten novocaine.

"No, because we're going to cut class. Come on."

We went to the student center. I rarely cut anything. But it seemed reasonable enough to sit with Cindy in a dark quiet corner behind one of the pillars instead of going to class.

"Your mother called my mother this morning after breakfast," said Cindy. "When your mom realized you spent the night on the couch because you were afraid to share a bedroom with Ashley, she knew she had to take action. They haven't found an institution for her yet, but you're going to come live with us until they do. You're going to have Elaine's room."

Cindy's family.

Warm, ordinary, loving. Mrs. Wethers adores making hot drinks for guests. Her sense of hospitality is completely dependent on hot drinks. She never would offer you ginger ale or Coke. It's always, "Susan! It's been ages! Hot chocolate? Coffee? Soup? Hot apple punch?" She watches while you drink, and it satisfies *her* more than you—she's solved your chill, your thirst, and your troubles.

"Okay," I said.

We sat silently for a long time. I couldn't get my thoughts straight enough to talk, so I didn't try.

"You know, it really hurt my feelings that you weren't coming to me to tell me everything," said Cindy. "I mean, what are best friends for? But I had a long talk with my parents last night."

There had been an awful lot of girls having long talks with their parents last night. Ashley, me, Shepherd, Cindy.

"And they said when things are really awful people close in on themselves like turtles. Keeping to yourself is protective."

"Oh, Cindy, there just didn't seem to be time to call you. All I could do was catch my breath and tread water."

"You don't have to tread water anymore. You'll be living with us."

I closed my eyes in relief. Just thinking of Mrs. Wethers and her fussy comforting attentions was a safety zone. Away from the place where teddy bears were stabbed and friends attacked and heirlooms desecrated. Cindy's house. A place to be cherished.

"You're such nice people," said Cindy. "I can't understand what's happening to you. You don't deserve it."

"I don't suppose deserving comes into it," I said. "There doesn't seem to be a system where you add up the good deeds and the bad deeds and get a life to fit."

"It's not fair!" said Cindy hotly.

"Speak to God about it, will you?"

We giggled. Mine was real. What a relief to be really laughing. To know that today after school I could go home to a real home. Passing bell rang and I got to my feet eagerly. Cindy had restored me.

She bounced off to her class and I headed for mine.

But cutting one class had changed me.

Given me ideas.

I thought, Why even bother with school today? I can't concentrate anyhow. I'll go home and pack and head for the Wethers' house and relax.

I telephoned, but nobody answered. My father would be at work. My mother? Ashley? Where would they be, together? I shrugged, went to the pay phone and called a taxi. I prefer to save my money for clothes, but this was an exceptional circumstance.

The taxi silently headed for Iron Mine Road. It was a beautiful day. Deep blue sky, one slim thread of white cloud, the maples turning color and the wind whipping through grass that needed one more mowing.

I paid the driver.

I got out, and the garage doors were open, which was wrong, and I wanted to tell the driver to wait, but he was already leaving. Iron Mine Road was far from any other fare. Our garage was once two sheds, leaning up against the kitchen. Two large swinging doors hang on black iron strap hinges. We never leave them open. The wind smacks them against the building with enough force to snap them off.

But they were open.

The pickup and the car were gone.

I stood by the lilacs. How stringy and ugly they looked with no leaves. The road was quiet. Nobody seemed to be home next door, either. I was alone on Iron Mine Road.

Telling myself not to be fanciful, I walked in by the garage, thinking I'd shut them from the inside and go into the house through the shed door, where the dryer and washing machine were. I pulled the doors closed. They creaked heavily, unwillingly, against the strong breeze. I walked into the shed.

Ashley was crouching on top of the dryer.

I gasped.

"What are you doing here?" she said irritably.

"Oh, hi," I said.

She was reaching for the deep high storage ledge. Pulling down a suitcase. The best one, the only leather one.

"You cutting class?" said Ashley. "That doesn't sound like you." She threw the suitcase to the floor. I jumped out of the way.

I felt out of kilter. *I* was the one who had come home to pack. Why was Ashley getting the suitcase? "Are you going somewhere?" I said.

"Yeah."

I digested this. "Where?"

"Don't know."

She began packing the suitcase. But not with clothing. With the silver teaspoons, the brass candlesticks, the pewter mugs, the collection of silver-handled mirrors. I wondered how much money she could get for all that. I wondered about the open garage doors. Was she expecting someone to come for her? Someone like Bob? Fear prickled my palms and my thighs. "Don't take that," I said. "Don't steal it, Ashley. Please don't do that."

"I need the money. You think Warren is going to give it to me? He gives you anything you want, because you're a malleable sweet darling little suburbanite. But me—nothing. All he wants is to lock me up."

"But he wouldn't want to lock you up if you didn't do things like this," I objected. "Ashley, don't steal this stuff. Please? Think about what you're doing."

Did I think we were going to open up a can of Campbell's soup together and sort out our problems over Chicken Noodle? Did I think she would clasp my hand in gratitude for showing her the light?

"Listen, Saint Susan. I do what I need to do. Don't get in my way."

Don't get in her way.

So what was I supposed to do? Go meekly away and pack my clothes while she packed my mother's treasures? Call the police? Dial 911, tell them last house on the right on Iron Mine Road, robbery in progress?

She was putting my radio into her suitcase. My good radio. My aunt and uncle bought it for me. The perfect size, the perfect weight. Terrific reception, good sound. "Give me my radio!" I yelled at her.

"Forget it."

I wrenched the radio out of her hands.

I walked into the kitchen, set it on the table, walked back out to the shed and retrieved an armload of silver. "You're not taking our things!" I yelled at her.

She stood there, amazed. I had never been anything but passive before. It shocked her. It was rare for Ash to be the one shocked. I rather liked it. I walked back out for another load. Ashley was holding the gasoline can we use to fill the lawnmower.

"See this?" she said, flicking the tiny red cap off the opening.

I froze.

She pulled out a pack of matches from her sweatshirt pocket. "See this?" she said, in a voice as soft as suffocation.

"Ash?" I whispered.

"Well named. You know what makes ashes? Fire does, Saint Susan. Fire."

She poured gasoline on my shoes.

For a time as long as nightmare I stood while my socks soaked up gasoline like a wick.

Ash struck the match.

I screamed and ran out of the shed, ripping back the latch on the garage doors. Ash ran after me, grabbing my jacket. She caught me, but the match had gone out. She had to light another one. I yanked open the garage doors and ran.

I ran down the drive and under the low sweeping branches of the ancient oak and past the stone walls. Past the chrysanthemum gardens and the lawns and the trikes on the grass. I didn't look back. Ash couldn't follow. She lacked the physical strength.

My sister.

My flesh and blood.

Ash is also a word from fire and brimstone.

Hell. Living hell.

She wanted fame so much she had surrendered everything else: goodness, kindness, decency, and love. They were not left in her soul. No matter how often we pretended and hoped, they were not there.

I ran and my chest cut like knives and my knees trembled and my calves knotted in cramps and I kept running. A horn honked. I jumped onto the verge to get out of the way, but the horn honked again.

I looked up. It was Whit.

No.

No.

Not now.

I had postured in the cafeteria and posed in the halls. Now, when my clothing was torn where I had jerked away from Ashley, when my shoes stank of gasoline and the wind had mangled my hair—now Whit saw me?

"You take up jogging?" yelled Whit. He was grinning at me. How handsome he was—leaning out of that window, he looked like a television idea of a teenage boy: dark and sexy and terrific.

My sister tried to murder me, I thought.

"You cutting class?" yelled Whit. He swung a U turn so he could pull up beside me. Still smiling, like the boy of any girl's dreams, he leaned over to open the passenger door for me.

FIFTEEN

"Call the police."

"I can't do that. She's my sister."

"How else you going to keep her from setting fire to the house? Or the dog? Or your mother?"

I began crying. Whit pulled me up against him, his arm warm and comforting and heavy. I would not have thought I could sob on the shoulder of the boy I had a crush on. With Anthony I'd have thought only of running mascara. With Whit I didn't think. I just accepted his comfort.

"Oh, Whit. We're living in hell."

"No. You aren't living in hell. Ashley is."

His embrace was comforting. "Whit," I asked, "what hell do you know?"

He looked at me.

"You talk as if you've been there."

"I have in a way." He looked away from me, down the road, seeing things.

"What sort of hell? Yours? Or somebody else's?"

"Family."

"Tell me about it."

"No," he said gently.

"Why not? Because it's too painful?"

"Because I don't know you very well," he told me. "Maybe someday. Not now."

"You know all there is to know about me," I pointed out. "You even know my own sister wanted to murder me."

He smiled. "I know a lot about Ashley. I don't know much about Susan."

Did he want to know? I tried to fathom his expression, but he was right. We didn't know each other very well.

"I have the advantage over you," said Whit. "Nobody is watching the Moroso family. Nobody cares what we do. You've got a town lined up to check out Ashley's progress."

"Or lack of it."

"Right. But mine is a real secret. Nobody knows."

"Does that make it easier?" I asked him.

He shrugged. "No tragedy is easy." He withdrew his arm, swung another U-ie and began driving back toward my house. *Tragedy.* What a heavy word. "Where are we going?" I said.

"Your house. If you don't want the police, you may want the fire department."

"Whit, she's—she's—"

"Truly dangerous. I know. I can handle it."

"Don't hurt her."

He said, "I'm a hundred pounds heavier than she is. I don't need to hurt her. I can just hold her."

I looked at the McLeans' house and I looked at the Boyds' but I didn't look at our house.

Whit said, "Relax, Susan. House is still standing. Dog's wandering around the front yard. No neighbors are wringing their hands."

I looked.

We turned into the driveway. The garage doors were open, moving slightly in the breeze.

My sister was kneeling on the garage floor, right in the oil patch where my mother's car is usually parked, the gasoline can next to her. Her right hand was on the gas can. Her left hand was over her eyes.

"Oh, Whit!" I screamed. "She's got gasoline in her eyes! She's hurt. Oh, God, call the ambulance."

I had long ceased to believe that God was around, but in desperation I was calling upon Him as much as upon Whit. Although I think I had a little more faith in Whit.

Whit got to my sister before I did. He knelt beside her, tilting her face up to see the damage. "What happened?" he said. His features and voice were expressionless as ever.

She didn't answer. She turned and looked at me. She hadn't gotten anything in her eyes. She had been sobbing. Thin, thin fingers stretched toward me. "Susan," she whispered. "Susan, I meant it. I was really going to do it. My little sister. *Oh, Susan.* I was really going to do it."

She began shuddering, the palsy of some dreadful disease. "I'm in some old black-and-white film," she cried. "Full of starts and stops. I can see my whole life out there, flickering, jagged. *Susan, hold on to me, please!* It's crushing me."

"Crushing you," I repeated. My eyes met Whit's. We remembered his tape: the sound of being dashed against impenetrable walls.

We were watching the tape.

I held her, as Whit had held me, and the act was the act of sisterhood, of flesh and blood, of love.

Whit said, "It's cold here. She'll freeze." He scooped her up easily and carried her into the house without noticeable effort. We went into the living room and tucked her on the couch and wrapped afghans around her. "Who is this?" said Ashley.

"Whit Moroso," I said.

"He's better than that other one," she said, closing her eyes.

The side door burst open. My parents came rushing into the house, calling my name, calling Ashley's, fear and horror in their throats. "Whose car is that?" they screamed. "Who is here? What has she done? Susan, why weren't you in school? We called and you were gone!"

"I'm sorry. I—I did a stupid thing."

They stood by the couch, trying to assess the situation and failing.

"Tell them what happened, Susan," said my sister.

I told them.

My mother sagged against Dad. Dad looked twenty years older.

My sister said, "Cherry Hill. I'll sign myself in. Call them now before I change my mind."

The room trembled with years of emotional history and agony.

"Quick, Daddy," said Ashley, smiling the first real smile I had ever seen on her face. "Before I get mad again. You don't know how quickly I get mad."

"I know exactly how quickly you get mad," said my father dryly, and they both laughed. Real laughs.

She had called him Daddy. Not Warren.

I held tight to her hand. It was surprisingly strong and rough. Startled, I glanced down. "I switched with Ashley," said Whit, grinning at me.

My mother looked at us strangely. "Uh—I feel a little confused," she said. "This is—uh—?"

"Whit Moroso. My friend. He's been a big help."

"It was terribly nice of you to stop," said my mother formally.

"Nah. I had an ulterior motive."

"Doesn't everybody?" said Ash.

Whit grinned at her. "Yeah, but mine was understandable. I was on my way to have a wisdom tooth pulled. This was a piece of cake in comparison."

"Me," said Ashley. "A piece of cake."

"Definitely." Whit stood up. "Got to run along. If I'm really lucky the dentist can still squeeze me in."

I walked him to his car.

"I think it'll be okay," he said to me. "Not easy. But okay."

I tried to say thank you, but my throat closed.

Whit paused with one foot in the car. "You know," he said, "when I'm in the lab, I feel as if *music* is in there with me. Music the *person*. Music like the ancient Greeks said: a goddess."

He flushed, made a face, and dropped to the driver's seat. He put his key in the ignition. But he didn't drive away. He was caught up in a thought and he had to express it. He tried syllable after syllable and discarded them before he spoke, struggling for a way to say what he wanted to say. "Ashley used music instead of loved music," he said finally. "I guess you can't get away with that. And she didn't."

I could not believe how well he understood: Whit who had never known or spoken to Ashley.

But then, Whit had known and spoken to Music.

I shivered with the intensity of wanting him. This boy who was so handsome behind his dark moodiness, who was not a delinquent at all but a savior for me. I said, "Whit—" but I could not find a way to express myself. I tried to touch him, but I couldn't quite bear it, because it would mean nothing to him and fire to me, so I tangled my fingers in my own hair, wishing it was his hair, dark and thick and curled on his collar.

"Susan . . ." he said slowly.

I wanted to reach out to him so much. To be in his arms when I could think about his arms, instead of thinking about a sister with hate in her heart.

An ambulance came up Iron Mine Road. No siren, but red lights flashing. "Hall residence?" queried the driver, stopping by us.

I gestured at my own house and he turned in the drive.

Whit pulled me toward him, my face in the window against his, our lips touching and then our hands on each other, hanging on to each other, not gently, but frantically. "I don't know why this is happening," said Whit. "I'm not your type."

"Let's try. One date."

His lips were still on my skin and my cheek vibrated when he answered. "How will your friends react? You

170

get seen with me and you're out of the Derek-Anthony-Pammy-Caitlin crowd before you ever get started."

"Ashley was right about one thing," I told him. "Anthony. He is a lightweight."

"What am I? A heavyweight?" he teased.

I gave him back his own words. "I don't know. I don't know you very well yet."

The ambulance attendants came back out. Ashley was on a stretcher, unmoving beneath white blankets. Perhaps they had sedated her. I saw my father talking to the attendants. I guessed he was arranging to meet the ambulance at the hospital.

"Don't cry, Susan," said Whit. "Every single time I've been around you, you've cried."

"My father calls my mother and me the Wet Duet."

Whit burst out laughing. "I don't date Weeping Singles. You have to promise to smile."

"And what do you promise?"

"I promise to be here Friday at eight."

The smile came by itself. Glowing with me, it lifted my heart.

"Now that's a smile," said Whit very softly.

Crush. It's a word for something temporary. Something that weights you down and makes it hard to breathe. I don't have a crush on you now, I thought. I just plain love you. Good old reliable love.

The ambulance left.

Whit kissed me once, slowly, and then, very slowly, followed the ambulance. Fifty feet away he stopped, looked back at me, and yelled, "Friday? Eight?"

"Friday," I yelled back. "Eight."

He disappeared.

I walked back to the house. It was a long walk. You could have measured it in miles. Or maybe years.

I looked at my parents again, and I loved them just as much as I ever had. Ashley's life had been jagged for ten years; mine, for two weeks. But we had all come through. Mistakes and failures—we had managed to stay a family.

"Are you going to date Whit?" said my mother.

"Yes. Friday at eight."

"You'll need some new clothes. What will you need?"

"Everything," I told her. "I'm going to be dating him for years. Going everywhere together."

"I like a girl with faith in herself," said my father.

We smiled at one another, and then we hugged.

I'm at home, I thought. And at peace.

May Ashley have the same one day.